THE FOLGER LIBRARY
SHAKESPEARE

Designed to make Shakespeare's classic plays available to the general reader, each edition contains a reliable text with modernized spelling and punctuation, scene-by-scene plot summaries, and explanatory notes clarifying obscure and obsolete expressions. An interpretive essay and accounts of Shakespeare's life and theater form an instructive preface to each play.

Louis B. Wright, General Editor, was the Director of the Folger Shakespeare Library from 1948 until his retirement in 1968. He is the author of *Middle-Class Culture in Elizabethan England, Religion and Empire, Shakespeare for Everyman,* and many other books and essays on the history and literature of the Tudor and Stuart periods.

Virginia Lamar, Assistant Editor, served as research assistant to the Director and Executive Secretary of the Folger Shakespeare Library from 1946 until her death in 1968. She is the author of *English Dress in the Age of Shakespeare* and *Travel and Roads in England,* and coeditor of William Strachey's *Historie of Travell into Virginia Britania.*

The Folger Library General Reader's Shakespeare

MUCH ADO
ABOUT NOTHING

by

WILLIAM
SHAKESPEARE

WASHINGTON SQUARE PRESS
PUBLISHED BY POCKET BOOKS

New York   London   Toronto   Sydney   Tokyo   Singapore

A Washington Square Press Publication of
POCKET BOOKS, a division of Simon & Schuster Inc.
1230 Avenue of the Americas, New York, NY 10020

ISBN: 0-671-50814-8

First Pocket Books printing June 1964

20   19   18   17   16   15

WASHINGTON SQUARE PRESS and WSP colophon are registered trademarks of Simon & Schuster Inc.

Printed in the U.S.A.

Preface

This edition of *Much Ado about Nothing* is designed
to make available a readable text of one of Shakespeare's early comedies. In the centuries since Shakespeare, many changes have occurred in the mean-
ings of words, and some clarification of Shakespeare's vocabulary may be helpful. To provide the
reader with necessary notes in the most accessible
format, we have placed them on the pages facing
the text that they explain. We have tried to make
these notes as brief and simple as possible. Prelim-
inary to the text we have also included a brief statement of essential information about Shakespeare
and his stage. Readers desiring more detailed information should refer to the books suggested in the
references, and if still further information is needed,
the bibliographies in those books will provide the
necessary clues to the literature of the subject.

The early texts of Shakespeare's plays provide
only scattered stage directions and no indications of
setting, and it is conventional for modern editors to
add these to clarify the action. Such additions, and
additions to entrances and exits, as well as many
indications of act and scene division, are placed in
square brackets.

All illustrations are from material in the Folger
Library collections.

L. B. W.

V. A. L.

August 15, 1963

Duel between Witty Lovers

In *Much Ado about Nothing* Shakespeare treats
a theme that he found congenial, the play of wit
between a sparkling and clever woman and a man
who is fascinated by her mind no less than by her
physical charms. Few other dramatists showed so
much appreciation of the feminine mind; Shakespeare's plays are filled with bright women who are
living personalities, women who use their intelligence to delight us without sacrificing their feminine charms to parade as bluestockings. What this
tells about Shakespeare's own taste in women we
can guess; what it tells about his personal life and
the feminine friends that he must have known remains a mystery never to be unraveled. It is un-
likely that he found the stimulation for his characterization of Portia and Beatrice back in Stratford.
But whatever the source of his inspiration, we must
rejoice at its manifestation in the creation of a gal-
lery of delightful and intelligent women of whom
Rosalind, Viola, Portia, and Beatrice are the favorites. Of these none has excelled Beatrice in the
pleasure that she has given readers and spectators
of the play.

Although structurally the sparring of Benedick

and Beatrice occupies the position of a subplot in relation to the main action of *Much Ado about Nothing*, Shakespeare lavished his major effort on their creation and our own interest in the play centers upon them. Whenever they are on stage the tension increases and the spectator sits forward to listen with new intentness. Without Benedick and Beatrice, the play would be colorless and inane.

The battle of the sexes is a theme as old as Adam and Eve and is an ancient convention of the stage. An excellent example in Greek comedy is Aristophanes' *Lysistrata*. In one of his earliest comedies, *The Taming of the Shrew*, Shakespeare contributed a rollicking farce to this literature. The *Shrew* was not understood by Victorian critics, who saw in it a "brutalization" of the relations between men and women. They did not realize that Shakespeare was representing farcically the combat of the sexes that he would treat intellectually in *Much Ado about Nothing*. The wit combat between two protagonists of opposite sex, best exemplified in Elizabethan drama in *Much Ado*, was carried to exaggerated extremes in later drama, notably in Congreve's *The Way of the World*, perhaps the best example of high comedy in the Restoration period. In the Restoration, wit took the place of the humor of incongruity.

But in the Elizabethan period, both wit and humor had equal importance in the drama, and in *Much Ado* Shakespeare exemplified in a high degree both forms of entertainment. The witty sallies of Benedick and Beatrice are in striking contrast to the comic characters who appear in Dogberry's train. Dogberry himself is a creation who has taken his place among the immortals of broad comedy. According to John Aubrey, the Restoration gossip who collected bits of information about sundry writers and figures of the preceding age, Shakespeare based his characterization of Dogberry on observations from life, an assertion not hard to accept, for we have all known some minion of the law who might be writ down an ass. "The humor of the constable in *Midsummer Night's Dream* [Aubrey's error for *Much Ado*], he happened to take at Grendon—I think it was Midsummer Night that he happened to lie there—in Bucks, which is the road from London to Stratford, and there was living that constable about 1642 when I first came to Oxford. Mr. Joseph Howe is of that parish and knew him. Ben Jonson and he did gather humors of men daily wherever they came." If Shakespeare did not listen to a constable at Grendon, he had observed somewhere one who gave him the idea for Dogberry, the prototype of the conventional but ever-amusing fumbling stage policeman, a character still in high favor on the movie and television screens. Shakespeare had another certain motive in creating Dogberry. He wanted to write an effective part for one of the most accomplished clowns of the Elizabethan stage, Will Kemp. We know this because in the first printed version of the play the name "Kemp" has been left as the prefix to some of the speeches of Dogberry.

The serious part of *Much Ado*, the ill-starred love story of Hero and Claudio, is hardly more than a background for the witty byplay of Benedick and Beatrice and the bumbling low comedy of Dogberry and the watch. Deliberately the dramatist sees to it that the audience is not overly concerned about Hero's fate, for early in the play he reveals that the key to her vindication is already in the hands of Dogberry's men. Such suspense as the serious plot achieves derives from the bewilderment of the audience over the stupidities of the constables in bringing the plotters against Hero's honor to justice.

The three principal elements in *Much Ado*—the wit combat of Benedick and Beatrice, the foolery of Dogberry and the watch, and the love story of Hero and Claudio—in a dramatist less skillful than Shakespeare might have been left disparate and disconnected. Many a play in the Elizabethan period had a comic underplot for the entertainment of the groundlings that had no visible relation to the main plot. But Shakespeare always managed to weave his subplots and main plots together to give them an organic unity, and he was never more successful than in *Much Ado*. Through the activities of Dogberry, the plot against Hero is revealed. The loyalty of Beatrice to Hero is made a means of relating even the witty dialogue with Benedick to the main action. Few scenes are more effective in the theatre than Act IV, Scene I, when Beatrice, at the height of Benedick's passionate declaration that he would do anything for her, snaps, "Kill Claudio." Shakespeare never leaves the audience wondering what Benedick and Beatrice have to do with Claudio and Hero. We are conscious throughout that we are seeing a closely knit drama that moves to its climax, though we may have guessed the conclusion.

The skill in construction displayed by Shakespeare in *Much Ado* has won the admiration of critics, who forgive him the lack of motivation for Hero's disgrace, the weak characterization of Claudio, the protagonist in the main plot, and other imperfections in making the characters credible. So moved was Swinburne by the contemplation of Shakespeare's skill in weaving his plot elements together that he declared that *Much Ado* had "absolute power of composition, faultless balance, and blameless rectitude of design."

Other critics, less carried away than Swinburne, have complained about the characterization of Don John, a spirit of seemingly unmotivated evil, of Claudio for his heartlessness, and of Leonato for being so credulous and simple. As for Don John, Shakespeare is employing the conventional type of malcontent, a type popular on the stage at the time. The stage malcontent appears in many plays in one form or another. Sometimes he is merely the contemplative type ready to rail on fortune, like Jaques in *As You Like It;* at other times, he is more sinister, like Edmund in *King Lear* and Don John in *Much*

Ado. But whatever the degree of this character's discontent with the world, the Elizabethan audience was familiar with him and was ready to believe him capable of all sorts of sinister actions. Don John was the veritable "Machiavel" who would not seem improbable to Shakespeare's audience. Nor would the actions of Claudio seem improbable to the Elizabethans. He behaved according to the book—and as some men in real life were known to have behaved.

Much Ado was written at a period in Shakespeare's career when he had already achieved a great success as a playwright. He had behind him such comedies as *The Comedy of Errors, The Taming of the Shrew, Two Gentlemen of Verona, Love's Labor's Lost,* and *The Merchant of Venice. Much Ado* was probably written about 1598 and performed soon afterward. It therefore came immediately after the highly successful two parts of *Henry IV* and before the historical sequel, *Henry V. Much Ado* reflects the maturity and sureness of touch that had come to Shakespeare with his increasing experience of life and the further development of his craft as a dramatist. Despite the potentially tragic elements in the Hero-Claudio story, the play maintains its lightness and gaiety. The author is careful never to let the spectator believe for a minute that the outcome of even the serious scenes will be anything but happy. Assured that no misfortune is going to happen to anyone, the spectator willingly abandons himself to the merry duel between Benedick and Beatrice and the comic episodes of the country constable and his posse. Nothing very profound is uttered by anyone, and the play is less lyrical and more prosy than most, but the dialogue is bright and gay and one leaves the theatre in a good humor. Nobody even bothers about the deserved punishment of the errant Borachio and the mastermind of the plot, Don John.

Much Ado about Nothing was a popular play from the beginning. When it was first printed in 1600 the title page declared that it "hath been sundry times publicly performed." It was one of fourteen plays performed at Whitehall during 1612-13 as part of the entertainment for the Princess Elizabeth and the Elector of the Palatinate. Leonard Digges, a translator and friend of Shakespeare's, in commendatory verses printed with Shakespeare's *Poems* in 1640, referred to the continued popularity of the play.

During the Restoration, the Benedick and Beatrice scenes were utilized in part by Sir William Davenant in *The Law against Lovers* (1662). In 1721 *Much Ado* was revived briefly at Lincoln's Inn Fields, but it did not regain its popularity until David Garrick's revival at Drury Lane in 1748 with himself as Benedick and a famous actress of the day, Hannah Pritchard, as Beatrice. Garrick regarded Benedick as one of his best roles and revived *Much Ado* at regular intervals as long as he was manager of Drury Lane. Both John Philip Kemble and Charles Kemble were popular Benedicks, and Mrs. Siddons' Beatrice was the talk of the day.

Much Ado was acted frequently during the late eighteenth and nineteenth centuries and has continued to find favor with modern audiences. At the beginning of the present century Ellen Terry gained great fame as Beatrice. Although this role requires extraordinary finesse, it has been a favorite with some of the greatest actresses.

From the time of Will Kemp, the first Dogberry, this role has also been a favorite with stage comedians. It too requires skill, for an incompetent actor can make the lines sound both flat and fatuous; but a talented comedian can make Dogberry one of the funniest of Shakespeare's characters.

The main plot of *Much Ado* was an old story when Shakespeare chose to dramatize it; indeed it goes back ultimately to Greek romance. Matteo Bandello used it as No. 22 of his *Novelle* (1554), and it appeared a little later in Belleforest's *Histoires Tragiques* (1569). In Ariosto's *Orlando Furioso* (1516) the episode of Ariodante and Genevra in Canto V retells the story. A dramatized version under this name was performed by the boys of the Merchant Taylors' School in London in 1583. Edmund Spenser used the story again in Book II of the *Faerie Queene* (1590). From precisely which source Shakespeare took the story remains in doubt. He might have read it in Sir John Harington's translation of *Orlando Furioso* (1591). Although wit combats are not unknown in other literature, as for example in Baldassare Castiglione's *Il Cortegiano*

(1528), it is unnecessary to seek a literary source for Benedick and Beatrice, for even if Shakespeare knew the relevant passages in Castiglione he made the play of wit between Benedick and Beatrice his own. And of course the comic scenes with Dogberry and the watch are his invention.

THE TEXT

Much Ado was first printed in a Quarto version in 1600. The Quarto is unusually accurate, though in a few places the speech prefixes leave the name of Kemp for Dogberry and Cowley for Verges, evidence, perhaps, that a playhouse text was used for printer's copy. It was not printed again until its inclusion in the First Folio of 1623. The present editors have used the Quarto version with corrections where necessary from the Folio.

THE AUTHOR

As early as 1598 Shakespeare was so well known as a literary and dramatic craftsman that Francis Meres, in his *Palladis Tamia: Wits Treasury*, referred in flattering terms to him as "mellifluous and honey-tongued Shakespeare," famous for his *Venus and Adonis*, his *Lucrece*, and "his sugared sonnets," which were circulating "among his private friends." Meres observes further that "as Plautus and Seneca are accounted the best for comedy and tragedy among the Latins, so Shakespeare among the English is the most excellent in both kinds for the stage," and he mentions a dozen plays that had made a name for Shakespeare. He concludes with the remark that "the Muses would speak with Shakespeare's fine filed phrase if they would speak English."

To those acquainted with the history of the Elizabethan and Jacobean periods, it is incredible that anyone should be so naïve or ignorant as to doubt the reality of Shakespeare as the author of the plays that bear his name. Yet so much nonsense has been written about other "candidates" for the plays that it is well to remind readers that no credible evidence that would stand up in a court of law has ever been adduced to prove either that Shakespeare did not write his plays or that anyone else wrote them. All the theories offered for the authorship of Francis Bacon, the Earl of Derby, the Earl of Oxford, the Earl of Hertford, Christopher Marlowe, and a score of other candidates are mere conjectures spun from the active imaginations of persons who confuse hypothesis and conjecture with evidence.

As Meres's statement of 1598 indicates, Shakespeare was already a popular playwright whose name carried weight at the box office. The obvious reputation of Shakespeare as early as 1598 makes the effort to prove him a myth one of the most absurd in the history of human perversity.

The anti-Shakespeareans talk darkly about a plot of vested interests to maintain the authorship of Shakespeare. Nobody has any vested interest in Shakespeare, but every scholar is interested in the truth and in the quality of evidence advanced by special pleaders who set forth hypotheses in place of facts.

The anti-Shakespeareans base their arguments upon a few simple premises, all of them false. These false premises are that Shakespeare was an unlettered yokel without any schooling, that nothing is known about Shakespeare, and that only a noble lord or the equivalent in background could have written the plays. The facts are that more is known about Shakespeare than about most dramatists of his day, that he had a very good education, acquired in the Stratford Grammar School, that the plays show no evidence of profound book learning, and that the knowledge of kings and courts evident in the plays is no greater than any intelligent young man could have picked up at second hand. Most anti-Shakespeareans are naïve and betray an obvious snobbery. The author of their favorite plays, they imply, must have had a college diploma framed and hung on his study wall like the one in their dentist's office, and obviously so great a writer must have had a title or some equally significant evidence of exalted social background. They forget that genius has a way of cropping up in unexpected places and that none of the great creative writers of the world got his inspiration in a college or university course.

William Shakespeare was the son of John Shakespeare of Stratford-upon-Avon, a substantial citizen of that small but busy market town in the center of the rich agricultural county of Warwick. John Shakespeare kept a shop, what we would call a general store; he dealt in wool and other produce and gradually acquired property. As a youth, John Shakespeare had learned the trade of glover and leather worker. There is no contemporary evidence that the elder Shakespeare was a butcher, though the anti-Shakespeareans like to talk about the ignorant "butcher's boy of Stratford." Their only evidence is a statement by gossipy John Aubrey, more than a century after William Shakespeare's birth, that young William followed his father's trade, and when he killed a calf, "he would do it in a high style and make a speech." We would like to believe the story true, but Aubrey is not a very credible witness.

John Shakespeare probably continued to operate a farm at Snitterfield that his father had leased. He married Mary Arden, daughter of his father's landlord, a man of some property. The third of their eight children was William, baptized on April 26, 1564, and probably born three days before. At least, it is conventional to celebrate April 23 as his birthday.

The Stratford records give considerable information about John Shakespeare. We know that he held several municipal offices including those of alderman and mayor. In 1580 he was in some sort of legal difficulty and was fined for neglecting a summons of the Court of Queen's Bench requiring him to appear at Westminster and be bound over to keep the peace.

As a citizen and alderman of Stratford, John Shakespeare was entitled to send his son to the grammar school free. Though the records are lost, there can be no reason to doubt that this is where young William received his education. As any student of the period knows, the grammar schools provided the basic education in Latin learning and literature. The Elizabethan grammar school is not to be confused with modern grammar schools. Many cultivated men of the day received all their formal education in the grammar schools. At the universities in this period a student would have received little training that would have inspired him to be a creative writer. At Stratford young Shakespeare would have acquired a familiarity with Latin and some little knowledge of Greek. He would have read Latin authors and become acquainted with the plays of Plautus and Terence. Undoubtedly, in this period of his life he received that stimulation to read and explore for himself the world of ancient and modern history which he later utilized in his plays. The youngster who does not acquire this type of intellectual curiosity *before* college days rarely develops as a result of a college course the kind of mind Shakespeare demonstrated. His learning in books was anything but profound, but he clearly had the probing curiosity that sent him in search of information, and he had a keenness in the observation of nature and of humankind that finds reflection in his poetry.

There is little documentation for Shakespeare's boyhood. There is little reason why there should be. Nobody knew that he was going to be a dramatist about whom any scrap of information would be prized in the centuries to come. He was merely an active and vigorous youth of Stratford, perhaps assisting his father in his business, and no Boswell bothered to write down facts about him. The most important record that we have is a marriage license issued by the Bishop of Worcester on November 27, 1582, to permit William Shakespeare to marry Anne Hathaway, seven or eight years his senior; furthermore, the Bishop permitted the marriage after reading the banns only once instead of three times, evidence of the desire for haste. The need was explained on May 26, 1583, when the christening of Susanna, daughter of William and Anne Shakespeare, was recorded at Stratford. Two years later, on February 2, 1585, the records show the birth of twins to the Shakespeares, a boy and a girl who were christened Hamnet and Judith.

What William Shakespeare was doing in Stratford during the early years of his married life, or when he went to London, we do not know. It has been conjectured that he tried his hand at schoolteaching, but that is a mere guess. There is a legend that he left Stratford to escape a charge of poaching in the park of Sir Thomas Lucy of Charlecote, but there is no proof of this. There is also a legend that when first he came to London he earned his living by holding horses outside a playhouse and presently was given employment inside, but there is nothing better than eighteenth-century hearsay for this. How Shakespeare broke into the London theatres as a dramatist and actor we do not know. But lack of information is not surprising, for Elizabethans did not write their autobiographies, and we know even less about the lives of many writers and some men of affairs than we know about Shakespeare. By 1592 he was so well established and popular that he incurred the envy of the dramatist and pamphleteer Robert Greene, who referred to him as an "upstart crow . . . in his own conceit the only Shake-scene in a country." From this time onward, contemporary allusions and references in legal documents enable the scholar to chart Shakespeare's career with greater accuracy than is possible with most other Elizabethan dramatists.

By 1594 Shakespeare was a member of the company of actors known as the Lord Chamberlain's Men. After the accession of James I, in 1603, the company would have the sovereign for their patron and would be known as the King's Men. During the period of its greatest prosperity, this company would have as its principal theatres the Globe and the Blackfriars. Shakespeare was both an actor and a shareholder in the company. Tradition has assigned him such acting roles as Adam in *As You Like It* and the Ghost in *Hamlet,* a modest place on the stage that suggests that he may have had other duties in the management of the company. Such conclusions, however, are based on surmise.

What we do know is that his plays were popular and that he was highly successful in his vocation. His first play may have been *The Comedy of Errors*, acted perhaps in 1591. Certainly this was one of his earliest plays. The three parts of *Henry VI* were acted sometime between 1590 and 1592. Critics are not in agreement about precisely how much Shakespeare wrote of these three plays. *Richard III* probably dates from 1593. With this play Shakespeare captured the imagination of Elizabethan audiences, then enormously interested in historical plays. With *Richard III* Shakespeare also gave an interpretation pleasing to the Tudors of the rise to power of the grandfather of Queen Elizabeth. From this time onward, Shakespeare's plays followed on the stage in rapid succession: *Titus Andronicus, The Taming of the Shrew, The Two Gentlemen of Verona, Love's Labor's Lost, Romeo and Juliet, Richard II, A Midsummer Night's Dream, King John, The Merchant of Venice, Henry IV (Parts 1 and 2), Much Ado about Nothing, Henry V, Julius Cæsar, As You Like It, Twelfth Night, Hamlet, The Merry Wives of Windsor, All's Well That Ends Well, Measure for Measure, Othello, King Lear,* and nine others that followed before Shakespeare retired completely, about 1613.

In the course of his career in London, he made enough money to enable him to retire to Stratford with a competence. His purchase on May 4, 1597, of New Place, then the second-largest dwelling in Stratford, a "pretty house of brick and timber," with a handsome garden, indicates his increasing prosperity. There his wife and children lived while he busied himself in the London theatres. The summer before he acquired New Place, his life was darkened by the death of his only son, Hamnet, a child of eleven. In May, 1602, Shakespeare purchased one hundred and seven acres of fertile farmland near Stratford and a few months later bought a cottage and garden across the alley from New Place. About 1611, he seems to have returned permanently to Stratford, for the next year a legal document refers to him as "William Shakespeare of Stratford-upon-Avon . . . gentleman." To achieve the desired appellation of gentleman, William Shakespeare had seen to it that the College of Heralds in 1596 granted his father a coat of arms. In one step he thus became a second-generation gentleman.

Shakespeare's daughter Susanna made a good match in 1607 with Dr. John Hall, a prominent and prosperous Stratford physician. His second daughter, Judith, did not marry until she was thirty-two years old, and then, under somewhat scandalous circumstances, she married Thomas Quiney, a Stratford vintner. On March 25, 1616, Shakespeare made his will, bequeathing his landed property to Susanna, £300 to Judith, certain sums to other relatives, and his second-best bed to his wife, Anne. Much has been made of the second-best bed, but the legacy probably indicates only that Anne liked that particular bed. Shakespeare, following the practice of the time, may have already arranged with Susanna for his wife's care. Finally, on April 23, 1616, the anniversary of his birth, William Shakespeare died, and he was buried on April 25 within the chancel of Trinity Church, as befitted an honored citizen. On August 6, 1623, a few months before the publication of the collected edition of Shakespeare's plays, Anne Shakespeare joined her husband in death.

THE PUBLICATION OF HIS PLAYS

During his lifetime Shakespeare made no effort to publish any of his plays, though eighteen appeared in print in single-play editions known as quartos. Some of these are corrupt versions known as "bad quartos." No quarto, so far as is known, had the author's approval. Plays were not considered "literature" any more than most radio and television scripts today are considered literature. Dramatists sold their plays outright to the theatrical companies and it was usually considered in the company's interest to keep plays from getting into print. To achieve a reputation as a man of letters, Shakespeare wrote his *Sonnets* and his narrative poems, *Venus and Adonis* and *The Rape of Lucrece*, but he probably never dreamed that his plays would establish his reputation as a literary genius. Only Ben Jonson, a man known for his colossal conceit, had the crust to call his plays *Works*, as he did when he published an edition in 1616. But men laughed at Ben Jonson.

After Shakespeare's death, two of his old colleagues in the King's Men, John Heminges and Henry Condell, decided that it would be a good thing to print, in more accurate versions than were then available, the plays already published and eighteen additional plays not previously published in quarto. In 1623 appeared *Mr. William Shakespeares Comedies, Histories, & Tragedies. Published according to the True Originall Copies. London. Printed by Isaac Iaggard and Ed. Blount.* This was the famous First Folio, a work that had the authority of Shakespeare's associates. The only play commonly attributed to Shakespeare that was omitted in the First Folio was *Pericles.* In their preface, "To the great Variety of Readers," Heminges and Condell state that whereas "you were abused with diverse stolen and surreptitious copies, maimed and deformed by the frauds and stealths of injurious impostors that exposed them, even those are now offered to your view cured and perfect of their limbs; and all the rest, absolute in their numbers, as he conceived them." What they used for printer's copy is one of the vexed problems of scholarship, and skilled bibliographers have devoted years of study to the question of the relation of the "copy" for the First Folio to Shakespeare's manuscripts. In some cases it is clear that the editors corrected printed quarto versions of the plays, probably by comparison with playhouse scripts. Whether these scripts were in Shakespeare's autograph is anybody's guess. No manuscript of any play in Shakespeare's handwriting has survived. Indeed, very few play manuscripts from this period by any author are extant. The Tudor and Stuart periods had not yet learned to prize autographs and authors' original manuscripts.

Since the First Folio contains eighteen plays not previously printed, it is the only source for these. For the other eighteen, which had appeared in quarto versions, the First Folio also has the authority of an edition prepared and overseen by Shakespeare's colleagues and professional associates. But since editorial standards in 1623 were far from strict, and Heminges and Condell were actors rather than editors by profession, the texts are sometimes careless. The printing and proofreading of the First Folio also left much to be desired, and some garbled passages have had to be corrected and emended. The "good quarto" texts have to be taken into account in preparing a modern edition.

Because of the great popularity of Shakespeare through the centuries, the First Folio has become a prized book, but it is not a very rare one, for it is estimated that 238 copies are extant. The Folger Shakespeare Library in Washington, D.C., has seventy-nine copies of the First Folio, collected by the founder, Henry Clay Folger, who believed that a collation of as many texts as possible would reveal significant facts about the text of Shakespeare's plays. Dr. Charlton Hinman, using an ingenious machine of his own invention for mechanical collating, has made many discoveries that throw light on Shakespeare's text and on printing practices of the day.

The probability is that the First Folio of 1623 had an edition of between 1,000 and 1,250 copies. It is believed that it sold for £1, which made it an expensive book, for £1 in 1623 was equivalent to something between $40 and $50 in modern purchasing power.

During the seventeenth century, Shakespeare was sufficiently popular to warrant three later editions in folio size, the Second Folio of 1632, the Third Folio of 1663–1664, and the Fourth Folio of 1685. The Third Folio added six other plays ascribed to Shakespeare, but these are apocryphal.

THE SHAKESPEAREAN THEATRE

The theatres in which Shakespeare's plays were performed were vastly different from those we know today. The stage was a platform that jutted out into the area now occupied by the first rows of seats on the main floor, what is called the "orchestra" in America and the "pit" in England. This platform had no curtain to come down at the ends of acts and scenes. And although simple stage properties were available, the Elizabethan theatre lacked both the machinery and the elaborate movable scenery of the modern theatre. In the rear of the platform stage was a curtained area that could be used as an inner room, a tomb, or any such scene that might be required. A balcony above this inner room, and perhaps balconies on the sides of the stage, could represent the upper deck of a ship, the entry to Juliet's room, or a prison window. A trap door in the stage provided an entrance for ghosts and devils from the nether regions, and a similar trap in the canopied structure over the stage, known as the "heavens," made it possible to let down angels on a rope. These primitive stage arrangements help to account for many elements in Elizabethan plays. For example, since there was no curtain, the dramatist frequently felt the necessity of writing into his play action to clear the stage at the ends of acts and scenes. The funeral march at the end of *Hamlet* is not there merely for atmosphere; Shakespeare had to get the corpses off the stage. The lack of scenery also freed the dramatist from undue concern about the exact location of his sets, and the physical relation of his various settings to each other did not have to be worked out with the same precision as in the modern theatre.

Before London had buildings designed exclusively for theatrical entertainment, plays were given in inns and taverns. The characteristic inn of the period had an inner courtyard with rooms opening onto balconies overlooking the yard. Players could set up their temporary stages at one end of the yard and audiences could find seats on the balconies out of the weather. The poorer sort could stand or sit on the cobblestones in the yard, which was open to the sky. The first theatres followed this construction, and throughout the Elizabethan period the large public theatres had a yard in front of the stage open to the weather, with two or three tiers of covered balconies extending around the theatre. This physical structure again influenced the writing of plays. Because a dramatist wanted the actors to be heard, he frequently wrote into his play orations that could be delivered with declamatory effect. He also provided spectacle, buffoonery, and broad jests to keep the riotous groundlings in the yard entertained and quiet.

In another respect the Elizabethan theatre differed greatly from ours. It had no actresses. All women's roles were taken by boys, sometimes recruited from the boys' choirs of the London churches. Some of these youths acted their roles with great skill and the Elizabethans did not seem to be aware of any incongruity. The first actresses on the professional English stage appeared after the Restoration of Charles II, in 1660, when exiled Englishmen brought back from France practices of the French stage.

London in the Elizabethan period, as now, was the center of theatrical interest, though wandering actors from time to time traveled through the country performing in inns, halls, and the houses of the nobility. The first professional playhouse, called simply the Theatre, was erected by James Burbage, father of Shakespeare's colleague Richard Burbage, in 1576 on lands of the old Holywell Priory adjacent to Finsbury Fields, a playground and park area just north of the city walls. It had the advantage of being outside the city's jurisdiction and yet was near enough to be easily accessible. Soon after the Theatre was opened, another playhouse called the Curtain was erected in the same neighborhood. Both of these playhouses had open courtyards and were probably polygonal in shape.

About the time the Curtain opened, Richard Farrant, Master of the Children of the Chapel Royal at Windsor and of St. Paul's, conceived the idea of opening a "private" theatre in the old monastery buildings of the Blackfriars, not far from St. Paul's Cathedral in the heart of the city. This theatre was ostensibly to train the choirboys in plays for presentation at court, but Farrant managed to present plays to paying audiences and achieved considerable success until aristocratic neighbors complained and had the theatre closed. This first Blackfriars Theatre was significant, however, because it popularized the boy actors in a professional way and it paved the way for a second theatre in the Blackfriars, which Shakespeare's company took over more than thirty years later. By the last years of the sixteenth century, London had at least six professional theatres and still others were erected during the reign of James I.

The Globe Theatre, the playhouse that most people connect with Shakespeare, was erected early in 1599 on the Bankside, the area across the Thames from the city. Its construction had a dramatic beginning, for on the night of December 28, 1598, James Burbage's sons, Cuthbert and Richard, gathered together a crew who tore down the old theatre in Holywell and carted the timbers across the river to a site that they had chosen for a new playhouse. The reason for this clandestine operation was a row with the landowner over the lease to the Holywell property. The site chosen for the Globe was another playground outside of the city's jurisdiction, a region of somewhat unsavory character. Not far away was the Bear Garden, an amphitheatre devoted to the baiting of bears and bulls. This was also the region occupied by many houses of ill fame licensed by the Bishop of Winchester and the source of substantial revenue to him. But it was easily accessible either from London Bridge or by means of the cheap boats operated by the London watermen, and it had the great advantage of being beyond the authority of the Puritanical aldermen of London, who frowned on plays because they lured apprentices from work, filled their heads with improper ideas, and generally exerted a bad influence. The aldermen also complained that the crowds drawn together in the theatre helped to spread the plague.

The Globe was the handsomest theatre up to its time. It was a large building, apparently octagonal in shape, and open like its predecessors to the sky in the center, but capable of seating a large audience in its covered balconies. To erect and operate the Globe, the Burbages organized a syndicate composed of the leading members of the dramatic company, of which Shakespeare was a member. Since it was open to the weather and depended on natural light, plays had to be given in the afternoon.

This caused no hardship in the long afternoons of an English summer, but in the winter the weather was a great handicap and discouraged all except the hardiest. For that reason, in 1608 Shakespeare's company was glad to take over the lease of the second Blackfriars Theatre, a substantial, roomy hall reconstructed within the framework of the old monastery building. This theatre was protected from the weather and its stage was artificially lighted by chandeliers of candles. This became the winter playhouse for Shakespeare's company and at once proved so popular that the congestion of traffic created an embarrassing problem. Stringent regulations had to be made for the movement of coaches in the vicinity. Shakespeare's company continued to use the Globe during the summer months. In 1613 a squib fired from a cannon during a performance of *Henry VIII* fell on the thatched roof and the Globe burned to the ground. The next year it was rebuilt.

London had other famous theatres. The Rose, just west of the Globe, was built by Philip Henslowe, a semiliterate denizen of the Bankside, who became one of the most important theatrical owners and producers of the Tudor and Stuart periods. What is more important for historians, he kept a detailed account book, which provides much of our information about theatrical history in his time. Another famous theatre on the Bankside was the Swan, which a Dutch priest, Johannes de Witt, visited in 1596. The crude drawing of the stage which he made was copied by his friend Arend van Buchell; it is one of the important pieces of contemporary evidence for theatrical construction. Among the other theatres, the Fortune, north of the city, on Golding Lane, and the Red Bull, even farther away from the city, off St. John's Street, were the most popular. The Red Bull, much frequented by apprentices, favored sensational and sometimes rowdy plays.

The actors who kept all of these theatres going were organized into companies under the protection of some noble patron. Traditionally actors had enjoyed a low reputation. In some of the ordinances they were classed as vagrants; in the phraseology of the time, "rogues, vagabonds, sturdy beggars, and common players" were all listed together as undesirables. To escape penalties often meted out to these characters, organized groups of actors managed to gain the protection of various personages of high degree. In the later years of Elizabeth's reign, a group flourished under the name of the Queen's Men; another group had the protection of the Lord Admiral and were known as the Lord Admiral's Men. Edward Alleyn, son-in-law of Philip Henslowe, was the leading spirit in the Lord Admiral's Men. Besides the adult companies, troupes of boy actors from time to time also enjoyed considerable popularity. Among these were the Children of Paul's and the Children of the Chapel Royal.

The company with which Shakespeare had a long association had for its first patron Henry Carey,

Lord Hunsdon, the Lord Chamberlain, and hence they were known as the Lord Chamberlain's Men. After the accession of James I, they became the King's Men. This company was the great rival of the Lord Admiral's Men, managed by Henslowe and Alleyn.

All was not easy for the players in Shakespeare's time, for the aldermen of London were always eager for an excuse to close up the Blackfriars and any other theatres in their jurisdiction. The theatres outside the jurisdiction of London were not immune from interference, for they might be shut up by order of the Privy Council for meddling in politics or for various other offenses, or they might be closed in time of plague lest they spread infection. During plague times, the actors usually went on tour and played the provinces wherever they could find an audience. Particularly frightening were the plagues of 1592–1594 and 1613 when the theatres closed and the players, like many other Londoners, had to take to the country.

Though players had a low social status, they enjoyed great popularity, and one of the favorite forms of entertainment at court was the performance of plays. To be commanded to perform at court conferred great prestige upon a company of players, and printers frequently noted that fact when they published plays. Several of Shakespeare's plays were performed before the sovereign, and Shakespeare himself undoubtedly acted in some of these plays.

Many readers will want suggestions for further reading about Shakespeare and his times. A few references will serve as guides to further study in the enormous literature on the subject. A simple and useful little book is Gerald Sanders, *A Shakespeare Primer* (New York, 1950). *A Companion to Shakespeare Studies*, edited by Harley Granville-Barker and G. B. Harrison (Cambridge, 1934) is a valuable guide. The most recent concise handbook of facts about Shakespeare is Gerald E. Bentley, *Shakespeare: A Biographical Handbook* (New Haven, 1961). More detailed but not so voluminous as to be confusing is Hazelton Spencer, *The Art and Life of William Shakespeare* (New York, 1940), which, like Sanders' and Bentley's handbooks, contains a brief annotated list of useful books on various aspects of the subject. The most detailed and scholarly work providing complete factual information about Shakespeare is Sir Edmund Chambers, *William Shakespeare: A Study of Facts and Problems* (2 vols., Oxford, 1930).

Among other biographies of Shakespeare, Joseph Quincy Adams, *A Life of William Shakespeare* (Boston, 1923) is still an excellent assessment of the essential facts and the traditional information, and Marchette Chute, *Shakespeare of London* (New York, 1949; paperback, 1957) stresses Shakespeare's life in the theatre.

The Shakespeare Quarterly, published by the

Shakespeare Association of America under the editorship of James G. McManaway, is recommended for those who wish to keep up with current Shakespearean scholarship and stage productions. The *Quarterly* includes an annual bibliography of Shakespeare editions and works on Shakespeare published during the previous year.

Two new biographies of Shakespeare have recently appeared. A. L. Rowse, *William Shakespeare: A Biography* (London, 1963; New York, 1964) provides an appraisal by a distinguished English historian, who dismisses the notion that somebody else wrote Shakespeare's plays as arrant nonsense that runs counter to known historical fact. Peter Quennell, *Shakespeare: A Biography* (Cleveland and New York, 1963) is a sensitive and intelligent survey of what is known and surmised of Shakespeare's life.

The question of the authenticity of Shakespeare's plays arouses perennial attention. The theory of hidden cryptograms in the plays is demolished by William F. and Elizebeth S. Friedman, *The Shakespearean Ciphers Examined* (New York, 1957). A succinct account of the various absurdities advanced to suggest the authorship of a multitude of candidates other than Shakespeare will be found in R. C. Churchill, *Shakespeare and His Betters* (Bloomington, Ind., 1959). Another recent discussion of the subject, *The Authorship of Shakespeare*, by James G. McManaway (Washington, D.C., 1962), presents the evidence from contemporary records to prove the identity of Shakespeare the actor-playwright with Shakespeare of Stratford.

Scholars are not in agreement about the details of playhouse construction in the Elizabethan period. John C. Adams presents a plausible reconstruction of the Globe in *The Globe Playhouse: Its Design and Equipment* (Cambridge, Mass., 1942; 2nd rev. ed., 1961). A description with excellent drawings based on Dr. Adams' model is Irwin Smith, *Shakespeare's Globe Playhouse: A Modern Reconstruction in Text and Scale Drawings* (New York, 1956). Other sensible discussions are C. Walter Hodges, *The Globe Restored* (London, 1953) and A. M. Nagler, *Shakespeare's Stage* (New Haven, 1958). Bernard Beckerman, *Shakespeare at the Globe, 1599-1609* (New Haven, 1962; paperback, 1962) discusses Elizabethan staging and acting techniques.

A sound and readable history of the early theatres is Joseph Quincy Adams, *Shakespearean Playhouses: A History of English Theatres from the Beginnings to the Restoration* (Boston, 1917). For detailed, factual information about the Elizabethan and seventeenth-century stages, the definitive reference works are Sir Edmund Chambers, *The Elizabethan Stage* (4 vols., Oxford, 1923) and Gerald E. Bentley, *The Jacobean and Caroline Stages* (5 vols., Oxford, 1941-1956).

Further information on the history of the theatre and related topics will be found in the following titles: T. W. Baldwin, *The Organization and Personnel of the Shakespearean Company* (Princeton,

1927); Lily Bess Campbell, *Scenes and Machines on the English Stage during the Renaissance* (Cambridge, 1923); Esther Cloudman Dunn, *Shakespeare in America* (New York, 1939); George C. D. Odell, *Shakespeare from Betterton to Irving* (2 vols., London, 1931); Arthur Colby Sprague, *Shakespeare and the Actors: The Stage Business in His Plays (1660-1905)* (Cambridge, Mass., 1944) and *Shakespearian Players and Performances* (Cambridge, Mass., 1953); Leslie Hotson, *The Commonwealth and Restoration Stage* (Cambridge, Mass., 1928); Alwin Thaler, *Shakspere to Sheridan: A Book about the Theatre of Yesterday and To-day* (Cambridge, Mass., 1922); George C. Branam, *Eighteenth-Century Adaptations of Shakespeare's Tragedies* (Berkeley, 1956); C. Beecher Hogan, *Shakespeare in the Theatre, 1701-1800* (Oxford, 1957); Ernest Bradlee Watson, *Sheridan to Robertson: A Study of the 19th-Century London Stage* (Cambridge, Mass., 1926); and Enid Welsford, *The Court Masque* (Cambridge, Mass., 1927).

A brief account of the growth of Shakespeare's reputation is F. E. Halliday, *The Cult of Shakespeare* (London, 1947). A more detailed discussion is given in Augustus Ralli, *A History of Shakespearian Criticism* (2 vols., Oxford, 1932; New York, 1958). Harley Granville-Barker, *Prefaces to Shakespeare* (5 vols., London, 1927-1948; 2 vols., London, 1958) provides stimulating critical discussion of the plays. An older classic of criticism is Andrew C. Bradley, *Shakespearean Tragedy: Lectures on Ham-*

let, Othello, King Lear, Macbeth (London, 1904; paperback, 1955). Sir Edmund Chambers, *Shakespeare: A Survey* (London, 1935; paperback, 1958) contains short, sensible essays on thirty-four of the plays, originally written as introductions to single-play editions.

For the history plays see Lily Bess Campbell, *Shakespeare's "Histories": Mirrors of Elizabethan Policy* (Cambridge, 1947); John Palmer, *Political Characters of Shakespeare* (London, 1945; 1961); E. M. W. Tillyard, *Shakespeare's History Plays* (London, 1948); Irving Ribner, *The English History Play in the Age of Shakespeare* (Princeton, 1947); and Max M. Reese, *The Cease of Majesty* (London, 1961).

The comedies are illuminated by the following studies: C. L. Barber, *Shakespeare's Festive Comedy* (Princeton, 1959); John Russell Brown, *Shakespeare and His Comedies* (London, 1957); H. B. Charlton, *Shakespearian Comedy* (London, 1938; 4th ed., 1949); W. W. Lawrence, *Shakespeare's Problem Comedies* (New York, 1931); and Thomas M. Parrott, *Shakespearean Comedy* (New York, 1949).

Further discussions of Shakespeare's tragedies, in addition to Bradley, already cited, are contained in H. B. Charlton, *Shakespearian Tragedy* (Cambridge, 1948); Willard Farnham, *The Medieval Heritage of Elizabethan Tragedy* (Berkeley, 1936) and *Shakespeare's Tragic Frontier: The World of His Final Tragedies* (Berkeley, 1950); and Harold

S. Wilson, *On the Design of Shakespearian Tragedy* (Toronto, 1957).

The "Roman" plays are treated in M. M. MacCallum, *Shakespeare's Roman Plays and Their Background* (London, 1910) and J. C. Maxwell, "Shakespeare's Roman Plays, 1900-1956," *Shakespeare Survey 10* (Cambridge, 1957), 1-11.

Kenneth Muir, *Shakespeare's Sources: Comedies and Tragedies* (London, 1957) discusses Shakespeare's use of source material. The sources themselves have been reprinted several times. Among old editions are John P. Collier (ed.), *Shakespeare's Library* (2 vols., London, 1850), Israel C. Gollancz (ed.), *The Shakespeare Classics* (12 vols., London, 1907-26), and W. C. Hazlitt (ed.), *Shakespeare's Library* (6 vols., London, 1875). A modern edition is being prepared by Geoffrey Bullough with the title *Narrative and Dramatic Sources of Shakespeare* (London and New York, 1957-). Four volumes, covering the sources for the comedies and histories, have been published to date (1963).

In addition to the second edition of *Webster's New International Dictionary*, which contains most of the unusual words used by Shakespeare, the following reference works are helpful: Edwin A. Abbott, *A Shakespearian Grammar* (London, 1872); C. T. Onions, *A Shakespeare Glossary* (2nd rev. ed., Oxford, 1925); and Eric Partridge, *Shakespeare's Bawdy* (New York, 1948; paperback, 1960).

Some knowledge of the social background of the period in which Shakespeare lived is important for a full understanding of his work. A brief, clear, and accurate account of Tudor history is S. T. Bindoff, *The Tudors*, in the Penguin series. A readable general history is G. M. Trevelyan, *The History of England*, first published in 1926 and available in numerous editions. The same author's *English Social History*, first published in 1942 and also available in many editions, provides fascinating information about England in all periods. Sir John Neale, *Queen Elizabeth* (London, 1935; paperback, 1957) is the best study of the great Queen. Various aspects of life in the Elizabethan period are treated in Louis B. Wright, *Middle-Class Culture in Elizabethan England* (Chapel Hill, N.C., 1935; reprinted Ithaca, N.Y., 1958). *Shakespeare's England: An Account of the Life and Manners of His Age*, edited by Sidney Lee and C. T. Onions (2 vols., Oxford, 1917), provides much information on many aspects of Elizabethan life. A fascinating survey of the period will be found in Muriel St. C. Byrne, *Elizabethan Life in Town and Country* (London, 1925; rev. ed., 1954; paperback, 1961).

The Folger Library is issuing a series of illustrated booklets entitled "Folger Booklets on Tudor and Stuart Civilization," printed and distributed by Cornell University Press. Published to date are the following titles:

Giles E. Dawson, *The Life of William Shakespeare*
John R. Hale, *The Art of War and Renaissance England*

Virginia A. LaMar, *English Dress in the Age of Shakespeare*

——, *Travel and Roads in England*

James G. McManaway, *The Authorship of Shakespeare*

Dorothy E. Mason, *Music in Elizabethan England*

Garrett Mattingly, *The "Invincible" Armada and Elizabethan England*

Boies Penrose, *Tudor and Early Stuart Voyaging*

Conyers Read, *The Government of England under Elizabeth*

Albert J. Schmidt, *The Yeoman in Tudor and Stuart England*

Lilly C. Stone, *English Sports and Recreations*

Craig R. Thompson, *The Bible in English, 1525-1611*

——, *The English Church in the Sixteenth Century*

——, *Schools in Tudor England*

——, *Universities in Tudor England*

Louis B. Wright, *Shakespeare's Theatre and the Dramatic Tradition.*

At intervals the Folger Library plans to gather these booklets in hardbound volumes. The first is *Life and Letters in Tudor and Stuart England, First Folger Series,* edited by Louis B. Wright and Virginia A. LaMar (published for the Folger Shakespeare Library by Cornell University Press, 1962). The volume contains eleven of the separate booklets.

Don Pedro, Prince of Aragon.
Don John, his bastard brother.
Claudio, a young lord of Florence.
Benedick, a young lord of Padua.
Leonato, Governor of Messina.
Balthasar, attendant on *Don Pedro*.
Borachio, } followers of *Don John*.
Conrade, }
Friar Francis.
Dogberry, a constable.
Verges, a headborough.
A Sexton.
A Boy.
Hero, daughter to *Leonato*.
Beatrice, niece to *Leonato*.
Margaret, } waiting gentlewomen attending on *Hero*.
Ursula, }
Messengers, Watch, Attendants, etc.

SCENE: *Messina*.]

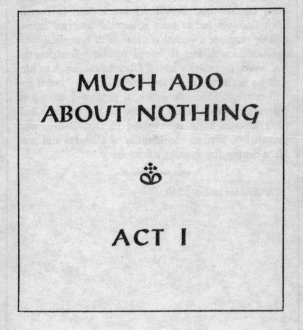

MUCH ADO
ABOUT NOTHING

❧

ACT I

I. i. Don Pedro of Aragon, returning to Messina from a victorious military engagement, is greeted by Leonato, Governor of Messina, his daughter Hero, and niece Beatrice. The Don and his company (including his half-brother Don John, and two young men, Claudio and Benedick) are invited to remain with Leonato for at least a month. Beatrice immediately resumes a verbal warfare with Benedick, who defends himself but is forced to allow Beatrice the last word. Benedick's friend Claudio confesses to him that he is charmed by Hero and will marry her if she will consent. Since Benedick, a professed enemy to marriage, cannot bring Claudio to his senses, Claudio's lovesick state is revealed to Don Pedro, who promises to assume the identity of Claudio and woo Hero during the evening's festivities.

7. **name:** noble birth.

ACT I

Scene I. [Before Leonato's house.]

Enter Leonato (Governor of Messina), Hero (his daughter), and Beatrice (his niece), with a Messenger.

Leon. I learn in this letter that Don Pedro of Aragon comes this night to Messina.

Mess. He is very near by this. He was not three leagues off when I left him.

Leon. How many gentlemen have you lost in this action? 5

Mess. But few of any sort, and none of name.

Leon. A victory is twice itself when the achiever brings home full numbers. I find here that Don Pedro hath bestowed much honor on a young Florentine 10 called Claudio.

Mess. Much deserved on his part, and equally rememb'red by Don Pedro. He hath borne himself beyond the promise of his age, doing in the figure of a lamb the feats of a lion. He hath indeed better 15 bett'red expectation than you must expect of me to tell you how.

I

22. **modest:** moderate; **badge of bitterness:** symbol of grief: tears.

26. **kind overflow of kindness:** natural overflow of emotion befitting a kinsman.

29. **Mountanto:** a fencing term, meaning an upright thrust. Beatrice implies that Benedick is a braggart.

37. **bills:** notices.

38. **at the flight:** to an archery contest.

39. **subscribed for:** signed in the name of.

40. **bird bolt:** a blunt arrow.

44. **tax:** criticize.

45. **be meet with you:** deal with you appropriately.

48. **holp:** obsolete past tense of "help."

Leon. He hath an uncle here in Messina will be very much glad of it.

Mess. I have already delivered him letters, and there appears much joy in him; even so much that joy could not show itself modest enough without a badge of bitterness.

Leon. Did he break out into tears?

Mess. In great measure.

Leon. A kind overflow of kindness. There are no faces truer than those that are so washed. How much better is it to weep at joy than to joy at weeping!

Beat. I pray you, is Signior Mountanto returned from the wars or no?

Mess. I know none of that name, lady. There was none such in the army of any sort.

Leon. What is he that you ask for, niece?

Hero. My cousin means Signior Benedick of Padua.

Mess. O, he's returned and as pleasant as ever he was.

Beat. He set up his bills here in Messina and challenged Cupid at the flight, and my uncle's fool, reading the challenge, subscribed for Cupid and challenged him at the bird bolt. I pray you, how many hath he killed and eaten in these wars? But how many hath he killed? For indeed I promised to eat all of his killing.

Leon. Faith, niece, you tax Signior Benedick too much; but he'll be meet with you, I doubt it not.

Mess. He hath done good service lady, in these wars.

Beat. You had musty victual, and he hath holp to

50. stomach: the word meant both "appetite" and "courage."

52. to: compared with.

57. mortal: imperfect.

63. five wits: common wit, imagination, fantasy, estimation, and memory were regarded as the five wits.

66. difference: sign of distinction (a heraldic term for a device to distinguish between branches of the same family).

76. and: if.

78. squarer: swashbuckler; one who delights in fighting.

eat it. He is a very valiant trencherman: he hath an
excellent stomach.   50

Mess. And a good soldier too, lady.

Beat. And a good soldier to a lady; but what is he
to a lord?

Mess. A lord to a lord, a man to a man; stuffed with
all honorable virtues.   55

Beat. It is so indeed. He is no less than a stuffed
man; but for the stuffing—well, we are all mortal.

Leon. You must not, sir, mistake my niece. There
is a kind of merry war betwixt Signior Benedick and
her. They never meet but there's a skirmish of wit be-   60
tween them.

Beat. Alas, he gets nothing by that! In our last con-
flict four of his five wits went halting off, and now is
the whole man governed with one; so that if he have
wit enough to keep himself warm, let him bear it for   65
a difference between himself and his horse; for it is
all the wealth that he hath left to be known a reason-
able creature. Who is his companion now? He hath
every month a new sworn brother.

Mess. Is't possible?   70

Beat. Very easily possible. He wears his faith but
as the fashion of his hat; it ever changes with the next
block.

Mess. I see, lady, the gentleman is not in your
books.   75

Beat. No; and he were, I would burn my study. But
I pray you, who is his companion? Is there no young
squarer now that will make a voyage with him to
the Devil?

84. **presently:** instantly.
86. **'a:** he.
99. **charge:** burden (of trouble and expense).
105. **have it full:** are fully answered.

A Spaniard of the sixteenth century. From Cesare Vecellio, *Habiti antichi et moderni di tutto il mondo* (1598).

4

Mess. He is most in the company of the right noble 80
Claudio.

Beat. O Lord, he will hang upon him like a disease!
He is sooner caught than the pestilence, and the taker
runs presently mad. God help the noble Claudio! If
he have caught the Benedick, it will cost him a thou- 85
sand pound ere 'a be cured.

Mess. I will hold friends with you, lady.

Beat. Do, good friend.

Leon. You will never run mad, niece.

Beat. No, not till a hot January. 90

Mess. Don Pedro is approached.

Enter Don Pedro, Claudio, Benedick, Balthasar,
and John the Bastard.

Pedro. Good Signior Leonato, are you come to meet
your trouble? The fashion of the world is to avoid
cost, and you encounter it.

Leon. Never came trouble to my house in the like- 95
ness of your Grace; for, trouble being gone, comfort
should remain; but when you depart from me, sorrow abides and happiness takes his leave.

Pedro. You embrace your charge too willingly. I
think this is your daughter. 100

Leon. Her mother hath many times told me so.

Bene. Were you in doubt, sir, that you asked her?

Leon. Signior Benedick, no; for then were you a
child.

Pedro. You have it full, Benedick. We may guess 105
by this what you are, being a man. Truly the lady

107. **fathers herself:** proclaims her father's name in her facial resemblance to him.

117. **meet:** suitable.

124. **dear:** great.

126. **for that:** with regard to courtship.

135–6. **bird of my tongue:** talking bird; **beast of yours:** dumb animal.

fathers herself. Be happy, lady; for you are like an honorable father.

Bene. If Signior Leonato be her father, she would not have his head on her shoulders for all Messina, as 110 like him as she is.

Beat. I wonder that you will still be talking, Signior Benedick. Nobody marks you.

Bene. What, my dear Lady Disdain! are you yet living? 115

Beat. Is it possible Disdain should die while she hath such meet food to feed it as Signior Benedick? Courtesy itself must convert to disdain if you come in her presence.

Bene. Then is courtesy a turncoat. But it is certain 120 I am loved of all ladies, only you excepted; and I would I could find in my heart that I had not a hard heart, for truly I love none.

Beat. A dear happiness to women! They would else have been troubled with a pernicious suitor. I thank 125 God and my cold blood, I am of your humor for that. I had rather hear my dog bark at a crow than a man swear he loves me.

Bene. God keep your Ladyship still in that mind! So some gentleman or other shall scape a predestinate 130 scratched face.

Beat. Scratching could not make it worse, and 'twere such a face as yours were.

Bene. Well, you are a rare parrot-teacher.

Beat. A bird of my tongue is better than a beast of 135 yours.

Bene. I would my horse had the speed of your

139. a: in.

140. a jade's trick: i.e., like an old nag, he cannot last out the contest.

150. Being reconciled: i.e., since he (John) is reconciled to Don Pedro.

151. duty: courtesy.

165. low: short.

tongue, and so good a continuer. But keep your way,
a God's name! I have done.

Beat. You always end with a jade's trick; I know 140
you of old.

Pedro. That is the sum of all, Leonato. Signior
Claudio and Signior Benedick, my dear friend Leonato hath invited you all. I tell him we shall stay here
at the least a month, and he heartily prays some occa- 145
sion may detain us longer. I dare swear he is no hypocrite but prays from his heart.

Leon. If you swear, my lord, you shall not be for-
sworn. [*To Don John*] Let me bid you welcome, my
lord. Being reconciled to the Prince your brother, I 150
owe you all duty.

John. I thank you. I am not of many words, but I
thank you.

Leon. Please it your Grace lead on?

Pedro. Your hand, Leonato; we will go together. 155
        Exeunt. Manent Benedick and Claudio.

Claud. Benedick, didst thou note the daughter of
Signior Leonato?

Bene. I noted her not, but I looked on her.

Claud. Is she not a modest young lady?

Bene. Do you question me, as an honest man should 160
do, for my simple true judgment? Or would you have
me speak after my custom, as being a professed tyrant
to their sex?

Claud. No; I pray thee speak in sober judgment.

Bene. Why, i' faith, methinks she's too low for a 165
high praise, too brown for a fair praise, and too little
for a great praise. Only this commendation I can af-

177–78. with a sad brow: earnestly; **flouting Jack:** mocking knave.

178–79. Cupid is a good hare-finder and Vulcan a rare carpenter: both statements would be false: Cupid is usually described as blind or blindfolded; Vulcan was an armorer and blacksmith.

180. go in the song: hold up a part in accordance with your mood.

191–92. wear his cap with suspicion: i.e., run the risk of acquiring the horns of a cuckold (man with unfaithful wife).

193. Go to: come, come!

194–95. wear the print of it and sigh away Sundays: let your servitude mark your weekly holiday with grief.

Vulcan at his forge. From Vincenzo Cartari, *Imagini delli dei de gl'antichi* (1674).

ford her, that were she other than she is, she were
unhandsome, and being no other but as she is, I do
not like her.   170

Claud. Thou thinkest I am in sport. I pray thee tell
me truly how thou likest her.

Bene. Would you buy her, that you inquire after
her?

Claud. Can the world buy such a jewel?   175

Bene. Yea, and a case to put it into. But speak you
this with a sad brow? Or do you play the flouting
Jack, to tell us Cupid is a good hare-finder and Vulcan a rare carpenter? Come, in what key shall a man
take you to go in the song?   180

Claud. In mine eye she is the sweetest lady that
ever I looked on.

Bene. I can see yet without spectacles, and I see no
such matter. There's her cousin, and she were not
possessed with a fury, exceeds her as much in beauty 185
as the first of May doth the last of December. But I
hope you have no intent to turn husband, have you?

Claud. I would scarce trust myself, though I had
sworn the contrary, if Hero would be my wife.

Bene. Is't come to this? In faith, hath not the 190
world one man but he will wear his cap with suspicion? Shall I never see a bachelor of threescore
again? Go to, i' faith! And thou wilt needs thrust thy
neck into a yoke, wear the print of it and sigh away
Sundays.   195

208. **so were it utt'red:** this is exactly the way Benedick would announce the fact.

209. **the old tale:** a popular version of the Bluebeard legend.

215. **fetch me in:** entrap me.

218. **two faiths and troths:** i.e., one owed to Claudio and one to Don Pedro.

Enter Don Pedro.

Look! Don Pedro is returned to seek you.

Pedro. What secret hath held you here, that you
followed not to Leonato's?

Bene. I would your Grace would constrain me to
tell.   200

Pedro. I charge thee on thy allegiance.

Bene. You hear, Count Claudio. I can be secret as
a dumb man, I would have you think so; but, on my
allegiance—mark you this—on my allegiance! He is in
love. With who? Now that is your Grace's part. Mark 205
how short his answer is: with Hero, Leonato's short
daughter.

Claud. If this were so, so were it utt'red.

Bene. Like the old tale, my lord: "It is not so, nor
'twas not so; but indeed, God forbid it should be so!" 210

Claud. If my passion change not shortly, God forbid it should be otherwise.

Pedro. Amen, if you love her; for the lady is very
well worthy.

Claud. You speak this to fetch me in, my lord.   215

Pedro. By my troth, I speak my thought.

Claud. And, in faith, my lord, I spoke mine.

Bene. And, by my two faiths and troths, my lord, I
spoke mine.

Claud. That I love her, I feel.   220

Pedro. That she is worthy, I know.

Bene. That I neither feel how she should be loved,
nor know how she should be worthy, is the opinion

226–27. **in the despite of:** in mocking.

232. **recheat:** series of notes on a horn; i.e., he will not have his cuckold state proclaimed by the horns on his forehead.

233. **hang my bugle in an invisible baldric:** be unable to conceal my horns.

236. **fine:** upshot.

237. **go the finer:** dress more finely (for not having the expense of a wife).

247. **argument:** example.

250. **Adam:** Adam Bell, an expert archer in an old ballad.

251. **try:** prove.

252. **"In time the savage bull doth bear the yoke":** an ancient proverb.

253. **sensible:** intelligent.

that fire cannot melt out of me. I will die in it at the
stake.   225

Pedro. Thou wast ever an obstinate heretic in the
despite of beauty.

Claud. And never could maintain his part but in the
force of his will.

Bene. That a woman conceived me, I thank her;   230
that she brought me up, I likewise give her most hum-
ble thanks; but that I will have a recheat winded in
my forehead, or hang my bugle in an invisible baldric,
all women shall pardon me. Because I will not do
them the wrong to mistrust any, I will do myself the   235
right to trust none; and the fine is (for the which I
may go the finer), I will live a bachelor.

Pedro. I shall see thee, ere I die, look pale with
love.

Bene. With anger, with sickness, or with hunger,   240
my lord; not with love. Prove that ever I lose more
blood with love than I will get again with drinking,
pick out mine eyes with a ballad-maker's pen and
hang me up at the door of a brothel house for the
sign of blind Cupid.   245

Pedro. Well, if ever thou dost fall from this faith,
thou wilt prove a notable argument.

Bene. If I do, hang me in a bottle like a cat and
shoot at me; and he that hits me, let him be clapped
on the shoulder and called Adam.   250

Pedro. Well, as time shall try:
"In time the savage bull doth bear the yoke."

Bene. The savage bull may; but if ever the sensible
Benedick bear it, pluck off the bull's horns and set

260. **horn-mad:** raving mad.

262. **in Venice:** notorious for its complaisant women.

264. **temporize with the hours:** alter with the passage of time.

266. **commend me to him:** give him my greetings.

271. **tuition:** supervision; protection.

276. **guarded:** trimmed.

278. **flout old ends:** mock snatches of wise sayings (with a pun on **old ends** meaning "cloth remnants").

The yoke of Matrimony. From Henry Peacham, *Minerva Britanna* (1612).

them in my forehead, and let me be vilely painted, 255
and in such great letters as they write "Here is good
horse to hire," let them signify under my sign "Here
you may see Benedick the married man."

Claud. If this should ever happen, thou wouldst be
horn-mad.   260

Pedro. Nay, if Cupid have not spent all his quiver
in Venice, thou wilt quake for this shortly.

Bene. I look for an earthquake too, then.

Pedro. Well, you will temporize with the hours. In
the meantime, good Signior Benedick, repair to 265
Leonato's, commend me to him and tell him I will not
fail him at supper; for indeed he hath made great
preparation.

Bene. I have almost matter enough in me for such
an embassage; and so I commit you—   270

Claud. To the tuition of God. From my house—if
I had it—

Pedro. The sixth of July. Your loving friend, Benedick.

Bene. Nay, mock not, mock not. The body of your 275
discourse is sometime guarded with fragments, and
the guards are but slightly basted on neither. Ere you
flout old ends any further, examine your conscience.
And so I leave you.   *Exit.*

Claud. My liege, your Highness now may do me 280
     good.

Pedro. My love is thine to teach. Teach it but how,
And thou shalt see how apt it is to learn
Any hard lesson that may do thee good.

Claud. Hath Leonato any son, my lord?   285

287. **affect:** incline to be in love with.

301. **break with:** inform.

307. **salved:** made it more palatable.

310. **The fairest grant is the necessity:** the very thing one needs is the finest gift to receive.

311. **Look what:** whatever; **'Tis once:** to sum up, this is the situation.

Pedro. No child but Hero; she's his only heir.
Dost thou affect her, Claudio?
   Claud.   O my lord,
When you went onward on this ended action,
I looked upon her with a soldier's eye,   290
That liked, but had a rougher task in hand
Than to drive liking to the name of love;
But now I am returned and that war-thoughts
Have left their places vacant, in their rooms
Come thronging soft and delicate desires,   295
All prompting me how fair young Hero is,
Saying I liked her ere I went to wars.
   Pedro. Thou wilt be like a lover presently
And tire the hearer with a book of words.
If thou dost love fair Hero, cherish it,   300
And I will break with her and with her father,
And thou shalt have her. Was't not to this end
That thou beganst to twist so fine a story?
   Claud. How sweetly you do minister to love,
That know love's grief by his complexion!   305
But lest my liking might too sudden seem,
I would have salved it with a longer treatise.
   Pedro. What need the bridge much broader than
     the flood?
The fairest grant is the necessity.   310
Look what will serve is fit. 'Tis once, thou lovest,
And I will fit thee with the remedy.
I know we shall have reveling tonight.
I will assume thy part in some disguise
And tell fair Hero I am Claudio,   315
And in her bosom I'll unclasp my heart

319. **break:** mention the matter.

▆▆▆▆▆▆▆▆▆▆▆▆▆▆▆▆▆▆▆▆▆▆▆▆▆▆

I. [ii.] Antonio, Leonato's brother, learns from one who overheard part of Don Pedro and Claudio's conversation that the Don is in love with Hero and plans to speak to her that evening. He reports this to Leonato, who is skeptical but resolves to prepare his daughter in case a declaration of love is forthcoming.

▆▆▆▆▆▆▆▆▆▆▆▆▆▆▆▆▆▆

1. **cousin:** kinsman.
5. **they:** the news (often a plural).
6. **As the event stamps them:** that is as the outcome may certify.
13. **top:** front lock; a reference to the proverb "Take Time by the forelock, for he is bald behind," i.e., there's no time like the present.

And take her hearing prisoner with the force
And strong encounter of my amorous tale.
Then after to her father will I break;
And the conclusion is, she shall be thine.   320
In practice let us put it presently.

Exeunt.

[Scene II. A room in Leonato's house.]

*Enter Leonato and [Antonio,] an old man, brother to
Leonato.*

Leon. How now, brother? Where is my cousin your
son? Hath he provided this music?

Ant. He is very busy about it. But, brother, I can
tell you strange news that you yet dreamt not of.

Leon. Are they good?   5

Ant. As the event stamps them; but they have a
good cover, they show well outward. The Prince and
Count Claudio, walking in a thick-pleached alley in
mine orchard, were thus much overheard by a man of
mine: the Prince discovered to Claudio that he loved   10
my niece your daughter and meant to acknowledge
it this night in a dance, and if he found her accordant,
he meant to take the present time by the top and
instantly break with you of it.

Leon. Hath the fellow any wit that told you this?   15

Ant. A good sharp fellow. I will send for him, and
question him yourself.

Leon. No, no. We will hold it as a dream till it ap-

23. **cry you mercy:** beg your pardon.

I. [iii.] Don John expresses his discontent to Conrade. Don Pedro has forgiven him a recent rebellion against his authority, but Don John chafes at what he considers some restrictions on his liberty and is more resentful than grateful for his brother's generosity. When Conrade tells him of Claudio's desire to marry Hero, Don John is hopeful that he may satisfy his jealousy of Claudio, who ranks high in Don Pedro's esteem, by thwarting the match.

1. **goodyear:** mischief.
2. **out of measure:** inappropriately.
8–9. **sufferance:** endurance.
11. **born under Saturn:** of a Saturnine (malevolent) disposition.
12. **mortifying mischief:** fatal malady.

The planet Saturn. From *Albumasar de magnis iunctionis* (1515).

13

pear itself; but I will acquaint my daughter withal,
that she may be the better prepared for an answer, if   20
peradventure this be true. Go you and tell her of it.
                                    [*Exit Antonio.*]

[*Enter Antonio's son with a Musician and others.*]

[*To the Son*] Cousin, you know what you have to do.
—[*To the Musician*] O, I cry you mercy, friend. Go
you with me, and I will use your skill.—Good cousin,
have a care this busy time.   25
                                    Exeunt.

[Scene III. Another room in Leonato's house.]

*Enter Don John the Bastard and Conrade, his
companion.*

Con. What the goodyear, my lord! Why are you
thus out of measure sad?
  John. There is no measure in the occasion that
breeds; therefore the sadness is without limit.
  Con. You should hear reason.   5
  John. And when I have heard it, what blessing
brings it?
  Con. If not a present remedy, at least a patient sufferance.
  John. I wonder that thou (being, as thou sayst thou   10
art, born under Saturn) goest about to apply a moral
medicine to a mortifying mischief. I cannot hide what

13. **sad:** grave.

16-7. **claw no man in his humor:** cater to no man's whim.

21. **grace:** favor.

25. **canker:** dog-rose (a wild variety).

27. **carriage:** style of behavior; **rob:** gain by false pretenses.

31. **enfranchised with a clog:** at liberty but hindered in my movements.

36. **use it only:** give it my full attention.

I am: I must be sad when I have cause and smile at
no man's jests; eat when I have stomach and wait for
no man's leisure; sleep when I am drowsy and tend on   15
no man's business; laugh when I am merry and claw
no man in his humor.

Con. Yea, but you must not make the full show of
this till you may do it without controlment. You have
of late stood out against your brother, and he hath   20
ta'en you newly into his grace, where it is impossible
you should take true root but by the fair weather that
you make yourself. It is needful that you frame the
season for your own harvest.

John. I had rather be a canker in a hedge than a   25
rose in his grace, and it better fits my blood to be dis-
dained of all than to fashion a carriage to rob love
from any. In this, though I cannot be said to be a
flattering honest man, it must not be denied but I am
a plain-dealing villain. I am trusted with a muzzle and   30
enfranchised with a clog; therefore I have decreed not
to sing in my cage. If I had my mouth, I would bite; if
I had my liberty, I would do my liking. In the meantime, let me be that I am, and seek not to alter me.

Con. Can you make no use of your discontent?   35
John. I make all use of it, for I use it only.

Enter Borachio.

Who comes here? What news, Borachio?
Bora. I came yonder from a great supper. The
Prince your brother is royally entertained by Leonato,

43. **What is he for a fool:** who is the fool.

45. **Marry:** verily (a mild exclamation or oath deriving from "by the Virgin Mary").

48. **proper:** fine (ironic).

52. **forward:** precocious; **March-chick:** fledgling.

54. **entertained for:** hired as.

55. **smoking:** fumigating with aromatic smoke.

56. **sad:** serious.

57. **arras:** tapestry hanging.

63. **sure:** faithful.

67–8. **o' my mind:** i.e., would think of poisoning the company.

68. **prove:** attempt.

69. **wait upon:** accompany.

and I can give you intelligence of an intended mar- 40
riage.

John. Will it serve for any model to build mischief
on? What is he for a fool that betroths himself to
unquietness?

Bora. Marry, it is your brother's right hand. 45

John. Who? the most exquisite Claudio?

Bora. Even he.

John. A proper squire! And who? and who? Which
way looks he?

Bora. Marry, on Hero, the daughter and heir of 50
Leonato.

John. A very forward March-chick! How came you
to this?

Bora. Being entertained for a perfumer, as I was
smoking a musty room, comes me the Prince and 55
Claudio, hand in hand in sad conference. I whipt me
behind the arras and there heard it agreed upon that
the Prince should woo Hero for himself and, having
obtained her, give her to Count Claudio.

John. Come, come, let us thither. This may prove 60
food to my displeasure. That young start-up hath all
the glory of my overthrow. If I can cross him any way,
I bless myself every way. You are both sure and will
assist me?

Con. To the death, my lord. 65

John. Let us to the great supper. Their cheer is the
greater that I am subdued. Would the cook were o'
my mind! Shall we go prove what's to be done?

Bora. We'll wait upon your Lordship.

Exeunt.

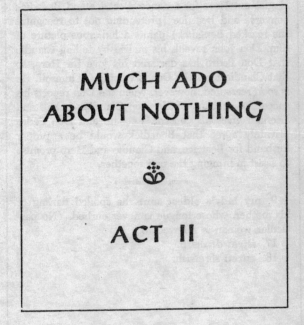

MUCH ADO
ABOUT NOTHING

❧

ACT II

II. [i.] Leonato has told Hero that Don Pedro may propose to her. With marriage so prominent in his thoughts, he rallies Beatrice about getting a husband, but she scoffs at the possibility of finding a suitable man. At the first opportunity, Don Pedro singles out Hero for a dance. Beatrice and Benedick converse and Beatrice (pretending not to recognize the masked Benedick) paints a ludicrous picture of him. Don John reveals his malice by telling Claudio that Don Pedro has declared his love for Hero, so that Claudio fears the Don is wooing for himself. He is soon reassured, however, when the Don reports his successful courting of Hero on Claudio's behalf and Leonato gives his consent. Leonato and Don Pedro privately agree that Benedick would be a proper husband for Beatrice, and Claudio and Hero promise to assist in bringing the pair together.

░░░░░░░░░░░░░░░░░░░░░░░░░░

9. **my lady's eldest son:** the spoiled darling of his mother, whose tongue is never curbed. (No particular woman is referred to.)

17. **shrewd:** sharp.

18. **curst:** shrewish.

ACT II

[Scene I. A hall in Leonato's house.]

Enter Leonato, [Antonio] his brother, Hero his daughter, and Beatrice his niece, a kinsman, [and Margaret and Ursula].

Leon. Was not Count John here at supper?

Ant. I saw him not.

Beat. How tartly that gentleman looks! I never can see him but I am heartburned an hour after.

Hero. He is of a very melancholy disposition. 5

Beat. He were an excellent man that were made just in the midway between him and Benedick. The one is too like an image and says nothing, and the other too like my lady's eldest son, evermore tattling.

Leon. Then half Signior Benedick's tongue in 10 Count John's mouth, and half Count John's melancholy in Signior Benedick's face—

Beat. With **a good leg** and a good foot, uncle, and money enough in his purse, such a man would win any woman in the world—if 'a could get her good will. 15

Leon. By my troth, niece, thou wilt never get thee a husband if thou be so shrewd of thy tongue.

Ant. In faith, she's too curst.

16

25. **Just:** exactly.

28. **lie in the woolen:** sleep in a bed without sheets, with the woolen blanket next my skin.

37–8. **in earnest:** in advance payment (of salary as the bearward's apprentice); **bearward:** a man who trained and exhibited bears, and might also have trained monkeys as part of his act; **lead his apes into hell:** i.e., be resigned to spinsterhood, a reference to the proverbial saying "Old maids lead apes in hell."

Beat. Too curst is more than curst. I shall lessen God's sending that way, for it is said, "God sends a curst cow short horns," but to a cow too curst He sends none.

Leon. So, by being too curst, God will send you no horns.

Beat. Just, if He send me no husband; for the which blessing I am at Him upon my knees every morning and evening. Lord I could not endure a husband with a beard on his face. I had rather lie in the woolen!

Leon. You may light on a husband that hath no beard.

Beat. What should I do with him? dress him in my apparel and make him my waiting gentlewoman? He that hath a beard is more than a youth, and he that hath no beard is less than a man; and he that is more than a youth is not for me; and he that is less than a man, I am not for him. Therefore I will even take sixpence in earnest of the bearward and lead his apes into hell.

Leon. Well then, go you into hell?

Beat. No; but to the gate, and there will the Devil meet me like an old cuckold with horns on his head, and say, "Get you to Heaven, Beatrice, get you to Heaven. Here's no place for you maids." So deliver I up my apes and away to St. Peter—for the Heavens. He shows me where the bachelors sit, and there live we as merry as the day is long.

Ant. [*To Hero*] Well, niece, I trust you will be ruled by your father.

Beat. Yes, faith. It is my cousin's duty to make

62. **in that kind:** regarding marriage. Leonato does not yet know that he woos for Claudio.

65–6. **important:** importunate.

66. **measure:** (1) moderation; (2) a dance step.

68. **measure:** slow and stately dance.

69. **cinquepace:** a lively dance.

71. **state and ancientry:** old-fashioned stateliness.

75. **passing shrewdly:** exceedingly sharply.

76–7. **see a church by daylight:** proverbial.

A stately measure. From Jehan Tabourot, *Orchesography* (1925 reprint).

curtsy and say, "Father, as it please you." But yet for   5(
all that, cousin, let him be a handsome fellow, or else
make another curtsy and say, "Father, as it please me."

Leon. Well, niece, I hope to see you one day fitted
with a husband.

Beat. Not till God make men of some other metal   5!
than earth. Would it not grieve a woman to be over-
mastered with a piece of valiant dust? to make an account of her life to a clod of wayward marl? No,
uncle, I'll none. Adam's sons are my brethren, and
truly I hold it a sin to match in my kindred.   6(

Leon. Daughter, remember what I told you. If the
Prince do solicit you in that kind, you know your
answer.

Beat. The fault will be in the music, cousin, if you
be not wooed in good time. If the Prince be too im-   6
portant, tell him there is measure in everything, and
so dance out the answer. For, hear me, Hero: wooing,
wedding, and repenting is as a Scotch jig, a measure,
and a cinquepace: the first suit is hot and hasty like a
Scotch jig—and full as fantastical; the wedding man-   7(
nerly modest, as a measure, full of state and ancientry;
and then comes Repentance and with his bad legs falls
into the cinquepace faster and faster, till he sink into
his grave.

Leon. Cousin, you apprehend passing shrewdly.   7!

Beat. I have a good eye, uncle; I can see a church
by daylight.

Leon. The revelers are ent'ring, brother, make good
room.   [*Exit Antonio.*]

81. **So:** provided that; **softly:** slowly.

87. **favor:** appearance; **defend:** forbid.

88. **case:** mask.

89. **visor:** mask; **Philemon:** an old countryman who, with his wife Baucis, offered Jove and Mercury hospitality when everyone else had refused them (Ovid, *Metamorphoses*, bk. viii).

103. **Answer, clerk:** i.e., say "Amen." Balthasar's responses have been like those of the parish clerk during Sunday service.

Philemon and Baucis. From Ovid, *Metamorphoses* (1602).

*Enter Don Pedro, Claudio, Benedick, Balthasar, [and
    Antonio, all masked]; Don John and Borachio.*

Pedro. Lady, will you walk about with your friend?   8

Hero. So you walk softly and look sweetly and say
nothing, I am yours for the walk; and especially when
I walk away.

Pedro. With me in your company?

Hero. I may say so when I please.   8

Pedro. And when please you to say so?

Hero. When I like your favor, for God defend the
lute should be like the case!

Pedro. My visor is Philemon's roof; within the
house is Jove.   ͼ

Hero. Why then, your visor should be thatched.

Pedro. Speak low, if you speak love.

                           [*Takes her aside.*]

Balth. Well, I would you did like me.

Marg. So would not I for your own sake, for I have
many ill qualities.   ͼ

Balth. Which is one?

Marg. I say my prayers aloud.

Balth. I love you the better. The hearers may cry
Amen.

Marg. God match me with a good dancer!   1ϲ

Balth. Amen.

Marg. And God keep him out of my sight when
the dance is done! Answer, clerk.

Balth. No more words. The clerk is answered.

                           [*Takes her aside.*]

107. **At a word:** to be brief.

110. **do him so ill-well:** imitate his infirmities so well.

111. **up and down:** to the life.

123. **the "Hundred Merry Tales":** a contemporary jestbook.

131. **Only his gift:** his only gift.

Urs. I know you well enough. You are Signior Antonio. 105

Ant. At a word, I am not.

Urs. I know you by the waggling of your head.

Ant. To tell you true, I counterfeit him.

Urs. You could never do him so ill-well unless you 110 were the very man. Here's his dry hand up and down. You are he, you are he!

Ant. At a word, I am not.

Urs. Come, come, do you think I do not know you by your excellent wit? Can virtue hide itself? Go to, 115 mum, you are he. Graces will appear, and there's an end.   [*They step aside.*]

Beat. Will you not tell me who told you so?

Bene. No, you shall pardon me.

Beat. Nor will you not tell me who you are? 120

Bene. Not now.

Beat. That I was disdainful, and that I had my good wit out of the "Hundred Merry Tales." Well, this was Signior Benedick that said so.

Bene. What's he? 125

Beat. I am sure you know him well enough.

Bene. Not I, believe me.

Beat. Did he never make you laugh?

Bene. I pray you, what is he?

Beat. Why, he is the Prince's jester, a very dull 130 fool. Only his gift is in devising impossible slanders. None but libertines delight in him; and the commendation is not in his wit but in his villainy; for he both pleases men and angers them, and then they

136. **fleet:** assembled company; **boarded:** accosted.

139. **break a comparison:** utter a satirical comment.

155–56. **very near my brother in his love:** i.e., a dear friend of my brother.

158. **honest:** honorable.

laugh at him and beat him. I am sure he is in the 135
fleet. I would he had boarded me.

Bene. When I know the gentleman, I'll tell him
what you say.

Beat. Do, do. He'll but break a comparison or two
on me; which peradventure, not marked or not 140
laughed at, strikes him into melancholy; and then
there's a partridge wing saved, for the fool will eat no
supper that night.   [*Music.*]
We must follow the leaders.

Bene. In every good thing.   145

Beat. Nay, if they lead to any ill, I will leave them
at the next turning.

*Dance. Exeunt [all but Don John, Borachio, and
Claudio].*

John. Sure my brother is amorous on Hero and hath
withdrawn her father to break with him about it. The
ladies follow her and but one visor remains.   150

Bora. And that is Claudio. I know him by his bearing.

John. Are not you Signior Benedick?

Claud. You know me well. I am he.

John. Signior, you are very near my brother in his 155
love. He is enamored on Hero. I pray you dissuade
him from her; she is no equal for his birth. You may
do the part of an honest man in it.

Claud. How know you he loves her?

John. I heard him swear his affection.   160

Bora. So did I too, and he swore he would marry
her tonight.

172. **faith melteth into blood:** loyalty is conquered by passion.

173. **accident of hourly proof:** happening demonstrated hourly.

179. **willow:** a common symbol for the pining lover.

180. **County:** Count.

Nobile ornata alle feste

Festive attire. From Cesare Vecellio, *Habiti antichi et moderni di tutto il mondo* (1598).

John. Come, let us to the banquet.

                   Exeunt. Manet Claudio.

  Claud. Thus answer I in name of Benedick

But hear these ill news with the ears of Claudio.   165

                      [Unmasks.]

'Tis certain so. The Prince woos for himself.

Friendship is constant in all other things,

Save in the office and affairs of love.

Therefore all hearts in love use their own tongues;

Let every eye negotiate for itself   170

And trust no agent; for beauty is a witch

Against whose charms faith melteth into blood.

This is an accident of hourly proof,

Which I mistrusted not. Farewell therefore Hero!

       Enter Benedick [unmasked].

  Bene. Count Claudio?   175

  Claud. Yea, the same.

  Bene. Come, will you go with me?

  Claud. Whither?

  Bene. Even to the next willow, about your own business, County. What fashion will you wear the 180 garland of? about your neck, like an usurer's chain? or under your arm, like a lieutenant's scarf? You must wear it one way, for the Prince hath got your Hero.

  Claud. I wish him joy of her.

  Bene. Why, that's spoken like an honest drovier. So 185 they sell bullocks. But did you think the Prince would have served you thus?

  Claud. I pray you leave me.

190. **post:** messenger bearing the news. This apparently echoes a tale in which the robbed man beats a post (pillar) instead of the thief.

191. **If it will not be:** if you won't leave me.

198. **puts the world into her person and so gives me out:** attributes her own opinion to everybody and so describes me.

202. **Troth:** on my oath.

203. **Lady Fame:** equivalent to Dame Rumor.

204. **warren:** a rabbit warren, which would be far from human dwellings.

211. **The flat transgression of a schoolboy:** a downright schoolboy's prank.

Bene. Ho! now you strike like the blind man! 'Twas the boy that stole your meat, and you'll beat the post. 190

Claud. If it will not be, I'll leave you.   *Exit.*

Bene. Alas, poor hurt fowl! now will he creep into sedges. But, that my Lady Beatrice should know me and not know me! The Prince's fool! Ha! it may be I go under that title because I am merry. Yea, but so I 195 am apt to do myself wrong. I am not so reputed. It is the base (though bitter) disposition of Beatrice that puts the world into her person and so gives me out. Well, I'll be revenged as I may.

Enter Don Pedro.

Pedro. Now, Signior, where's the Count? Did you 200 see him?

Bene. Troth, my lord, I have played the part of Lady Fame. I found him here as melancholy as a lodge in a warren. I told him, and I think I told him true, that your Grace had got the good will of this 205 young lady, and I off'red him my company to a willow tree, either to make him a garland, as being forsaken, or to bind him up a rod, as being worthy to be whipped.

Pedro. To be whipped? What's his fault? 210

Bene. The flat transgression of a schoolboy who, being overjoyed with finding a bird's nest, shows it his companion, and he steals it.

Pedro. Wilt thou make a trust a transgression? The transgression is in the stealer. 215

Bene. Yet it had not been amiss the rod had been

223–24. If their singing answer your saying, by my faith, you say honestly: i.e., I will credit your honesty if Hero does learn from you to respond to Claudio's love.

233. a great thaw: a period when a spring thaw results in muddy and impassable roads and everyone must stay at home.

234. impossible conveyance: unbelievable deftness.

235. at a mark: acting as a target.

237. terminations: descriptive terms.

241. have turned spit: forced him to perform the function of a turnspit, a menial occupation.

243. Ate: a goddess whose function was to foment discord.

244. conjure: exorcise her as though she were an evil spirit.

Hercules. From Vincenzo Cartari, *Imagini de gli dei delli antichi* (1615).

made, and the garland too; for the garland he might
have worn himself, and the rod he might have bestowed on you, who, as I take it, have stol'n his bird's
nest.   220

Pedro. I will but teach them to sing and restore
them to the owner.

Bene. If their singing answer your saying, by my
faith, you say honestly.

Pedro. The Lady Beatrice hath a quarrel to you.   225
The gentleman that danced with her told her she is
much wronged by you.

Bene. O, she misused me past the endurance of a
block! An oak but with one green leaf on it would
have answered her; my very visor began to assume   230
life and scold with her. She told me, not thinking I
had been myself, that I was the Prince's jester, that I
was duller than a great thaw, huddling jest upon jest
with such impossible conveyance upon me that I stood
like a man at a mark, with a whole army shooting at   235
me. She speaks poniards, and every word stabs. If her
breath were as terrible as her terminations, there were
no living near her; she would infect to the North Star.
I would not marry her though she were endowed with
all that Adam had left him before he transgressed. She   240
would have made Hercules have turned spit, yea, and
have cleft his club to make the fire too. Come, talk not
of her. You shall find her the infernal Ate in good
apparel. I would to God some scholar would conjure
her, for certainly, while she is here, a man may live as   245
quiet in hell as in a sanctuary, and people sin upon

254. **Prester John:** a legendary emperor, whose dominion was variously located in the Far East or Ethiopia; **Great Cham:** the Khan of Tartary, or Mongolia.

265. **use:** interest.

purpose, because they would go thither; so indeed all
disquiet, horror, and perturbation follows her.

Enter Claudio and Beatrice, Leonato, Hero.

Pedro. Look, here she comes.

Bene. Will your Grace command me any service to 250
the world's end? I will go on the slightest errand now
to the Antipodes that you can devise to send me on; I
will fetch you a toothpicker now from the furthest
inch of Asia; bring you the length of Prester John's
foot; fetch you a hair off the Great Cham's beard; do 255
you any embassage to the Pygmies—rather than hold
three words' conference with this harpy. You have no
employment for me?

Pedro. None, but to desire your good company.

Bene. O God, sir, here's a dish I love not! I cannot 260
endure my Lady Tongue.   *Exit.*

Pedro. Come, lady, come; you have lost the heart of
Signior Benedick.

Beat. Indeed, my lord, he lent it me awhile, and I
gave him use for it—a double heart for his single one. 265
Marry, once before he won it of me with false dice;
therefore your Grace may well say I have lost it.

Pedro. You have put him down, lady; you have put
him down.

Beat. So I would not he should do me, my lord, lest 270
I should prove the mother of fools. I have brought
Count Claudio, whom you sent me to seek.

Pedro. Why, how now, Count? Wherefore are you
sad?

279. **civil:** sober, with a pun on "Seville orange."

281. **blazon:** description.

282. **conceit:** imagination.

288–89. **all grace say Amen to it:** may Heaven favor it.

302–3. **Good Lord, for alliance:** a mock appeal to Heaven for a husband; **goes . . . to the world:** marries.

303. **sunburnt:** i.e., not fair enough to win a man.

Claud. Not sad, my lord.　　　　　　　　　　275

Pedro. How then? sick?

Claud. Neither, my lord.

Beat. The Count is neither sad, nor sick, nor merry, nor well; but civil Count—civil as an orange, and something of that jealous complexion.　　　　　　280

Pedro. I' faith, lady, I think your blazon to be true; though I'll be sworn, if he be so, his conceit is false. Here, Claudio, I have wooed in thy name, and fair Hero is won. I have broke with her father and his good will obtained. Name the day of marriage, and 285 God give thee joy!

Leon. Count, take of me my daughter, and with her my fortunes. His Grace hath made the match, and all grace say Amen to it!

Beat. Speak, Count, 'tis your cue.　　　　　290

Claud. Silence is the perfectest herald of joy. I were but little happy if I could say how much. Lady, as you are mine, I am yours. I give away myself for you and dote upon the exchange.

Beat. Speak, cousin; or, if you cannot, stop his 295 mouth with a kiss and let not him speak neither.

Pedro. In faith, lady, you have a merry heart.

Beat. Yea, my lord; I thank it, poor fool, it keeps on the windy side of care. My cousin tells him in his ear that he is in her heart.　　　　　　　　　　300

Claud. And so she doth, cousin.

Beat. Good Lord, for alliance! Thus goes every one to the world but I, and I am sunburnt. I may sit in a corner and cry Heigh-ho for a husband!

Pedro. Lady Beatrice, I will get you one.　　305

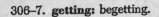

306–7. **getting:** begetting.

Beat. I would rather have one of your father's getting. Hath your Grace ne'er a brother like you? Your father got excellent husbands, if a maid could come by them.

Pedro. Will you have me, lady? 310

Beat. No, my lord, unless I might have another for working days: your Grace is too costly to wear every day. But I beseech your Grace, pardon me: I was born to speak all mirth and no matter.

Pedro. Your silence most offends me, and to be 315 merry best becomes you, for out o' question you were born in a merry hour.

Beat. No, sure, my lord, my mother cried; but then there was a star danced, and under that was I born. Cousins, God give you joy! 320

Leon. Niece, will you look to those things I told you of?

Beat. I cry you mercy, uncle. By your Grace's pardon. *Exit.*

Pedro. By my troth, a pleasant-spirited lady. 325

Leon. There's little of the melancholy element in her, my lord. She is never sad but when she sleeps, and not ever sad then; for I have heard my daughter say she hath often dreamt of unhappiness and waked herself with laughing. 330

Pedro. She cannot endure to hear tell of a husband.

Leon. O, by no means! She mocks all her wooers out of suit.

Pedro. She were an excellent wife for Benedick.

Leon. O Lord, my lord! if they were but a week 335 married they would talk themselves mad.

345. breathing: delay.

353–54. ten nights' watchings: ten sleepless nights.

359. unhopefulest: least suitable.

361. strain: either "heritage" or "character"; **approved:** demonstrated.

365. practice on: trick.

Cupid, the archer. From Achille Bocchi, *Symbolicarum quaestionum* (1555).

Pedro. County Claudio, when mean you to go to
church?

Claud. Tomorrow, my lord. Time goes on crutches
till love have all his rites.   340

Leon. Not till Monday, my dear son, which is hence
a just sevennight; and a time too brief, too, to have
all things answer my mind.

Pedro. Come, you shake the head at so long a
breathing; but I warrant thee, Claudio, the time shall 345
not go dully by us. I will in the interim undertake one
of Hercules' labors, which is, to bring Signior Benedick and the Lady Beatrice into a mountain of affection the one with the other. I would fain have it a
match, and I doubt not but to fashion it if you three 350
will but minister such assistance as I shall give you
direction.

Leon. My lord, I am for you, though it cost me ten
nights' watchings.

Claud. And I, my lord.   355

Pedro. And you too, gentle Hero?

Hero. I will do any modest office, my lord, to help
my cousin to a good husband.

Pedro. And Benedick is not the unhopefulest husband that I know. Thus far can I praise him: he is of 360
a noble strain, of approved valor, and confirmed
honesty. I will teach you how to humor your cousin
that she shall fall in love with Benedick; and I,
[*To Leonato and Claudio*] with your two helps, will
so practice on Benedick that, in despite of his quick 365
wit and his queasy stomach, he shall fall in love with
Beatrice. If we can do this, Cupid is no longer an

II. [ii.] Don John, displeased at the imminent marriage of Claudio and Hero, is comforted by Borachio, who proposes a plan to discredit Hero by staging a midnight meeting with her attendant, Margaret, dressed in her clothing. When Don Pedro and Claudio hear Borachio call Margaret by Hero's name as she stands at Hero's chamber window, they will be convinced that Hero is unchaste and Claudio will cast her off.

⁙⁙⁙⁙⁙⁙⁙⁙⁙⁙⁙⁙⁙⁙⁙⁙⁙⁙⁙⁙⁙⁙⁙⁙⁙⁙

5. **med'cinable:** curative.
19. **temper:** compound.
22. **estimation:** reputation.

archer; his glory shall be ours, for we are the only
love-gods. Go in with me, and I will tell you my drift.

Exeunt.

[Scene II. A hall in Leonato's house.]

Enter [Don] John and Borachio.

John. It is so. The Count Claudio shall marry the
daughter of Leonato.

Bora. Yea, my lord; but I can cross it.

John. Any bar, any cross, any impediment will be
med'cinable to me. I am sick in displeasure to him,   5
and whatsoever comes athwart his affection ranges
evenly with mine. How canst thou cross this marriage?

Bora. Not honestly, my lord, but so covertly that no
dishonesty shall appear in me.

John. Show me briefly how.   10

Bora. I think I told your Lordship, a year since, how
much I am in the favor of Margaret, the waiting gentlewoman to Hero.

John. I remember.

Bora. I can, at any unseasonable instant of the night,   15
appoint her to look out at her lady's chamber window.

John. What life is in that to be the death of this
marriage?

Bora. The poison of that lies in you to temper. Go
you to the Prince your brother; spare not to tell him   20
that he hath wronged his honor in marrying the re-
nowned Claudio (whose estimation do you mightily

23. **hold up:** praise; **stale:** strumpet.

25. **misuse:** deceive.

30. **meet:** convenient.

35. **cozened:** cheated.

45. **jealousy shall be called assurance:** suspicion shall become certainty.

47. **Grow this to what adverse issue it can:** no matter how disastrous the outcome of this may be.

52. **presently:** immediately.

hold up) to a contaminated stale, such a one as Hero.

John. What proof shall I make of that?

Bora. Proof enough to misuse the Prince, to vex 25
Claudio, to undo Hero, and kill Leonato. Look you for
any other issue?

John. Only to despite them I will endeavor anything.

Bora. Go then; find me a meet hour to draw Don 30
Pedro and the Count Claudio alone; tell them that
you know that Hero loves me; intend a kind of zeal
both to the Prince and Claudio, as—in love of your
brother's honor, who hath made this match, and his
friend's reputation, who is thus like to be cozened 35
with the semblance of a maid—that you have discovered thus. They will scarcely believe this without trial.
Offer them instances, which shall bear no less likelihood than to see me at her chamber window, hear me
call Margaret Hero, hear Margaret term me Claudio; 40
and bring them to see this the very night before the
intended wedding (for in the meantime I will so
fashion the matter that Hero shall be absent), and
there shall appear such seeming truth of Hero's dis-
loyalty that jealousy shall be called assurance and all 45
the preparation overthrown.

John. Grow this to what adverse issue it can, I will
put it in practice. Be cunning in the working this and
thy fee is a thousand ducats.

Bora. Be you constant in the accusation and my 50
cunning shall not shame me.

John. I will presently go learn their day of marriage.

Exeunt.

II. [iii.] Don Pedro, Claudio, and Leonato stage a conversation for Benedick's benefit in which they pretend concern at Beatrice's avowed passion for Benedick. They see no happiness for her in such a love, since her pride will not allow her to confess affection for one whom she has always scorned and whose mocking attitude toward women guarantees that he will spurn her. They sadly conclude that Beatrice should conquer her passion as best she can. Benedick, completely taken in, is abashed at being described as proud and self-centered. He resolves that if Beatrice loves him, her love shall be requited.

░░░░░░░░░░░░░░░░░░░░░░░░░

5. I am here already: i.e., no sooner said than done.

9. dedicates his behaviors to love: is entirely preoccupied with his role as lover.

11. argument: subject.

14. the tabor and the pipe: symbolic of peace. A **tabor** is a small drum.

19. orthography: i.e., orthographer, a word-fancier.

[Scene III. Leonato's orchard.]

Enter Benedick, alone.

Bene. Boy!

[*Enter Boy.*]

Boy. Signior?

Bene. In my chamber window lies a book. Bring it hither to me in the orchard.

Boy. I am here already, sir.   5

Bene. I know that, but I would have thee hence and here again. (*Exit Boy.*) I do much wonder that one man, seeing how much another man is a fool when he dedicates his behaviors to love, will, after he hath laughed at such shallow follies in others, become the   10 argument of his own scorn by falling in love; and such a man is Claudio. I have known when there was no music with him but the drum and the fife; and now had he rather hear the tabor and the pipe. I have known when he would have walked ten mile afoot to   15 see a good armor, and now will he lie ten nights awake carving the fashion of a new doublet. He was wont to speak plain and to the purpose, like an honest man and a soldier; and now is he turned orthography: his words are a very fantastical banquet—just so many   20 strange dishes. May I be so converted and see with these eyes? I cannot tell; I think not. I will not be

28. **come in my grace:** earn my favor.

30. **cheapen her:** bargain for her hand.

31–2. **noble, or not I for an angel:** a **noble** and an **angel** were both coins, the **angel** being worth half a pound, the **noble** a third of a pound.

38. **grace:** honor.

41. **We'll fit the kid fox with a pennyworth:** we'll give the clever young lad his money's worth.

44. **slander:** disgrace.

45. **the witness still of excellency:** always the proof of excellence.

46. **put a strange face on:** refuse to acknowledge.

sworn but love may transform me to an oyster; but
I'll take my oath on it, till he have made an oyster of
me, he shall never make me such a fool. One woman   25
is fair, yet I am well; another is wise, yet I am well;
another virtuous, yet I am well; but till all graces be in
one woman, one woman shall not come in my grace.
Rich she shall be, that's certain; wise, or I'll none; virtuous, or I'll never cheapen her; fair, or I'll never look   30
on her; mild, or come not near me; noble, or not I for
an angel; of good discourse, an excellent musician,
and her hair shall be of what color it please God. Ha,
the Prince and Monsieur Love! I will hide me in the
arbor.   [*Hides.*]   35

Enter *Don Pedro, Leonato, Claudio.*
Music [*within*].

Pedro. Come, shall we hear this music?
Claud. Yea, my good lord. How still the evening is,
As hushed on purpose to grace harmony!
Pedro. See you where Benedick hath hid himself?
Claud. O, very well, my lord. The music ended,   40
We'll fit the kid fox with a pennyworth.

Enter *Balthasar with Music.*

Pedro. Come, Balthasar, we'll hear that song again.
Balth. O, good my lord, tax not so bad a voice
To slander music any more than once.
Pedro. It is the witness still of excellency   45
To put a strange face on his own perfection.

57. crotchets: (1) quarter notes; (2) quibbles.
71. mo: more.

I pray thee sing, and let me woo no more.

   Balth. Because you talk of wooing, I will sing,
Since many a wooer doth commence his suit
To her he thinks not worthy, yet he woos,   50
Yet will he swear he loves.

   Pedro.   Nay, pray thee come;
Or if thou wilt hold longer argument,
Do it in notes.

   Balth.   Note this before my notes: 55
There's not a note of mine that's worth the noting.

   Pedro. Why, these are very crotchets that he speaks!
Note notes, forsooth, and nothing!   [*Music.*]

   Bene. [*Aside*] Now divine air! Now is his soul
ravished! Is it not strange that sheep's guts should   60
hale souls out of men's bodies? Well, a horn for my
money, when all's done.   [*Balthasar sings.*]

The Song.

Sigh no more, ladies, sigh no more!
   Men were deceivers ever,
One foot in sea and one on shore;   65
   To one thing constant never.
     Then sigh not so, but let them go,
   And be you blithe and bonny,
Converting all your sounds of woe
   Into Hey nonny, nonny.   70

Sing no more ditties, sing no mo,
   Of dumps so dull and heavy!

74. **leavy:** leafy.
79. **shift:** makeshift.
83. **night raven:** the raven's voice was considered an ill omen.

The fraud of men was ever so,
　　Since summer first was leavy.
　　　　Then sigh not so, &c.   75

Pedro. By my troth, a good song.

Balth. And an ill singer, my lord.

Pedro. Ha, no, no, faith! Thou singest well enough
for a shift.

Bene. [*Aside*] And he had been a dog that should   80
have howled thus, they would have hanged him; and
I pray God his bad voice bode no mischief. I had as
lief have heard the night raven, come what plague
could have come after it.

Pedro. Yea, marry. Dost thou hear, Balthasar? I   85
pray thee get us some excellent music; for tomorrow
night we would have it at the Lady Hero's chamber
window.

Balth. The best I can, my lord.

Pedro. Do so. Farewell.   90

　　　　　　　　Exit Balthasar [*with Musicians*].
Come hither, Leonato. What was it you told me of
today? that your niece Beatrice was in love with
Signior Benedick?

Claud. O, ay!—[*Aside to Pedro*] Stalk on, stalk on;
the fowl sits.—I did never think that lady would have   95
loved any man.

Leon. No, nor I neither; but most wonderful that
she should so dote on Signior Benedick, whom she
hath in all outward behaviors seemed ever to abhor.

Bene. [*Aside*] Is't possible? Sits the wind in that   100
corner?

109. **discovers:** reveals.

113. **sit you:** i.e., simply sit (the ethical dative construction).

121. **gull:** hoax.

123. **such reverence:** a man so worthy of respect.

124–25. **Hold it up:** carry on the deception.

Leon. By my troth, my lord, I cannot tell what to
think of it but that she loves him with an enraged
affection. It is past the infinite of thought.

Pedro. Maybe she doth but counterfeit.   105

Claud. Faith, like enough.

Leon. O God, counterfeit? There was never counterfeit of passion came so near the life of passion as she
discovers it.

Pedro. Why, what effects of passion shows she?   110

Claud. [*Aside*] Bait the hook well! This fish will
bite.

Leon. What effects, my lord? She will sit you—you
heard my daughter tell you how.

Claud. She did indeed.   115

Pedro. How, how, I pray you? You amaze me. I
would have thought her spirit had been invincible
against all assaults of affection.

Leon. I would have sworn it had, my lord—especially against Benedick.   120

Bene. [*Aside*] I should think this a gull but that the
white-bearded fellow speaks it. Knavery cannot, sure,
hide himself in such reverence.

Claud. [*Aside*] He hath ta'en the infection. Hold it
up.   125

Pedro. Hath she made her affection known to Benedick?

Leon. No, and swears she never will. That's her
torment.

Claud. 'Tis true indeed. So your daughter says.   130
"Shall I," says she, "that have so oft encount'red him
with scorn, write to him that I love him?"

135. **smock:** chemise.
153. **ecstasy:** passion.
160. **alms:** act of charity.
161–62. **out of all suspicion:** beyond question.

Leon. This says she now when she is beginning to
write to him; for she'll be up twenty times a night, and
there will she sit in her smock till she have writ a   135
sheet of paper. My daughter tells us all.

Claud. Now you talk of a sheet of paper, I remember a pretty jest your daughter told us of.

Leon. O, when she had writ it and was reading it
over, she found "Benedick" and "Beatrice" between   140
the sheet?

Claud. That.

Leon. O, she tore the letter into a thousand half-
pence, railed at herself that she should be so immodest
to write to one that she knew would flout her. "I   145
measure him," says she, "by my own spirit; for I
should flout him if he writ to me. Yea, though I love
him, I should."

Claud. Then down upon her knees she falls, weeps,
sobs, beats her heart, tears her hair, prays, curses—"O   150
sweet Benedick! God give me patience!"

Leon. She doth indeed; my daughter says so. And
ecstasy hath so much overborne her that my daughter
is something afeard she will do a desperate outrage
to herself. It is very true.   155

Pedro. It were good that Benedick knew of it by
some other, if she will not discover it.

Claud. To what end? He would make but a sport of
it and torment the poor lady worse.

Pedro. And he should, it were an alms to hang him!   160
She's an excellent sweet lady, and (out of all suspicion) she is virtuous.

Claud. And she is exceeding wise.

166. **blood:** passion.
170. **daffed:** discarded; **respects:** considerations.
178. **crossness:** quarrelsomeness.
179. **tender:** offer.
181. **contemptible:** contemptuous.
182. **proper:** handsome.
183. **good outward happiness:** fine appearance.
184. **Before God:** as God is my witness.

Pedro. In everything but in loving Benedick.

Leon. O, my lord, wisdom and blood combating in 165
so tender a body, we have ten proofs to one that blood
hath the victory. I am sorry for her, as I have just
cause, being her uncle and her guardian.

Pedro. I would she had bestowed this dotage on me.
I would have daffed all other respects and made her 170
half myself. I pray you tell Benedick of it and hear
what 'a will say.

Leon. Were it good, think you?

Claud. Hero thinks surely she will die; for she says
she will die if he love her not, and she will die ere she 175
make her love known, and she will die if he woo her,
rather than she will bate one breath of her accus-
tomed crossness.

Pedro. She doth well. If she should make tender of
her love, 'tis very possible he'll scorn it; for the man 180
(as you know all) hath a contemptible spirit.

Claud. He is a very proper man.

Pedro. He hath indeed a good outward happiness.

Claud. Before God! and in my mind, very wise.

Pedro. He doth indeed show some sparks that are 185
like wit.

Claud. And I take him to be valiant.

Pedro. As Hector, I assure you; and in the managing
of quarrels you may say he is wise, for either he avoids
them with great discretion or undertakes them with a 190
most Christianlike fear.

Leon. If he do fear God, 'a must necessarily keep
peace. If he break the peace, he ought to enter into a
quarrel with fear and trembling.

196. **large:** broad; ribald.

199. **wear it out:** overcome it.

212. **one:** each.

215. **a dumb show:** i.e., neither will be able to think of what to say.

217–18. **conference was sadly borne:** conversation was seriously carried on.

219–20. **her affections have their full bent:** she feels the utmost passion of which she is capable.

Pedro. And so will he do; for the man doth fear 195
God, howsoever it seems not in him by some large
jests he will make. Well, I am sorry for your niece.
Shall we go seek Benedick and tell him of her love?

Claud. Never tell him, my lord. Let her wear it out
with good counsel. 200

Leon. Nay, that's impossible; she may wear her
heart out first.

Pedro. Well, we will hear further of it by your
daughter. Let it cool the while. I love Benedick well,
and I could wish he would modestly examine himself 205
to see how much he is unworthy so good a lady.

Leon. My lord, will you walk? Dinner is ready.

                        [*They walk away.*]

Claud. If he do not dote on her upon this, I will
never trust my expectation.

Pedro. Let there be the same net spread for her, 210
and that must your daughter and her gentlewomen
carry. The sport will be when they hold one an
opinion of another's dotage, and no such matter.
That's the scene that I would see, which will be
merely a dumb show. Let us send her to call him in 215
to dinner.

            Exeunt [*Don Pedro, Claudio, and Leonato*].

Bene. This can be no trick. The conference was
sadly borne; they have the truth of this from Hero;
they seem to pity the lady. It seems her affections
have their full bent. Love me? Why, it must be re- 220
quited. I hear how I am censured. They say I will
bear myself proudly if I perceive the love come from
her. They say too that she will rather die than give any

228. **reprove:** disprove.
235. **sentences:** maxims (Latin *sententiae*).
237. **career of his humor:** course his inclination
suggests.

sign of affection. I did never think to marry. I must
not seem proud. Happy are they that hear their de- 225
tractions and can put them to mending. They say the
lady is fair—'tis a truth, I can bear them witness; and
virtuous—'tis so, I cannot reprove it; and wise, but for
loving me—by my troth, it is no addition to her wit,
nor no great argument of her folly, for I will be hor- 230
ribly in love with her. I may chance have some odd
quirks and remnants of wit broken on me because I
have railed so long against marriage. But doth not the
appetite alter? A man loves the meat in his youth that
he cannot endure in his age. Shall quips and sentences 235
and these paper bullets of the brain awe a man from
the career of his humor? No, the world must be peo-
pled. When I said I would die a bachelor, I did not
think I should live till I were married.

Enter Beatrice.

Here comes Beatrice. By this day, she's a fair lady! I 240
do spy some marks of love in her.

Beat. Against my will I am sent to bid you come in
to dinner.

Bene. Fair Beatrice, I thank you for your pains.

Beat. I took no more pains for those thanks than 245
you take pains to thank me. If it had been painful, I
would not have come.

Bene. You take pleasure then in the message?

Beat. Yea, just so much as you may take upon a
knife's point and choke a daw withal. You have no 250
stomach, signior. Fare you well. *Exit.*

Bene. Ha! "Against my will I am sent to bid you come in to dinner." There's a double meaning in that. "I took no more pains for those thanks than you took pains to thank me." That's as much as to say, "Any pains that I take for you is as easy as thanks." If I do not take pity of her, I am a villain; if I do not love her, I am a Jew. I will go get her picture. 255

Exit.

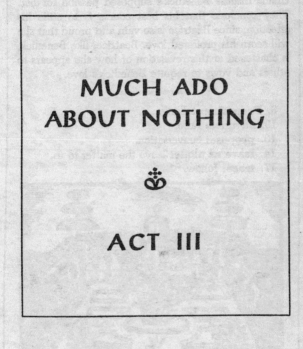

MUCH ADO
ABOUT NOTHING

❧

ACT III

III. [i.] Hero is simultaneously plotting to entrap Beatrice in the same manner. As Beatrice, informed by Margaret that she is a topic of conversation, conceals herself to eavesdrop, Hero and her attendant Ursula discuss Benedick's supposed passion for her. They conclude that his best course is to stifle his affection, since Beatrice is so vain and proud that she will scorn his proffered love. Beatrice, like Benedick, is chastened at this revelation of how she appears to others and vows to requite Benedick's love.

3. **Proposing:** talking.
10. **advance:** raise.
13. **propose:** conversation.
14. **leave us alone:** leave the matter to us.
17. **trace:** follow.

A pleached bower. From Henry Peacham, *Minerva Britanna* (1612).

ACT III

[Scene I. Leonato's garden.]

*Enter Hero and two gentlewomen, Margaret and
Ursula.*

Hero. Good Margaret, run thee to the parlor.
There shalt thou find my cousin Beatrice
Proposing with the Prince and Claudio.
Whisper her ear and tell her I and Ursley
Walk in the orchard and our whole discourse 5
Is all of her. Say that thou overheardst us;
And bid her steal into the pleached bower,
Where honeysuckles, ripened by the sun,
Forbid the sun to enter—like favorites,
Made proud by princes, that advance their pride 10
Against that power that bred it. There will she hide
   her
To listen our propose. This is thy office.
Bear thee well in it and leave us alone.
   Marg. I'll make her come, I warrant you, presently. 15
                                          [*Exit.*]

   Hero. Now, Ursula, when Beatrice doth come,
As we do trace this alley up and down,
Our talk must only be of Benedick.

22. **this matter:** material of this sort.
39. **haggards:** wild hawks.

When I do name him, let it be thy part
To praise him more than ever man did merit.   20
My talk to thee must be how Benedick
Is sick in love with Beatrice. Of this matter
Is little Cupid's crafty arrow made,
That only wounds by hearsay.

                    Enter Beatrice, [behind].

                              Now begin;   25
For look where Beatrice, like a lapwing, runs
Close by the ground to hear our conference.
    Urs. The pleasant'st angling is to see the fish
Cut with her golden oars the silver stream
And greedily devour the treacherous bait.   30
So angle we for Beatrice, who even now
Is couched in the woodbine coverture.
Fear you not my part of the dialogue.
    Hero. Then go we near her, that her ear lose noth-
        ing   35
Of the false sweet bait that we lay for it.
                    [They approach the arbor.]
No, truly, Ursula, she is too disdainful.
I know her spirits are as coy and wild
As haggards of the rock.
    Urs.   But are you sure   40
That Benedick loves Beatrice so entirely?
    Hero. So says the Prince and my new-trothed lord.
    Urs. And did they bid you tell her of it, madam?
    Hero. They did entreat me to acquaint her of it;
But I persuaded them, if they loved Benedick,   45

59. take no shape nor project of affection: form any conception of what love is like.

60. self-endeared: in love with herself.

66. spell him backward: turn his graces into faults.

68. black: dark complexioned; **antic:** grotesque figure.

70. agate: agate stone. Figures were sometimes carved in such stones to set in rings.

75. simpleness: sincerity; **purchaseth:** earn.

To wish him wrestle with affection
And never to let Beatrice know of it.
   Urs. Why did you so? Doth not the gentleman
Deserve as full, as fortunate a bed
As ever Beatrice shall couch upon?   50
   Hero. O god of love! I know he doth deserve
As much as may be yielded to a man;
But Nature never framed a woman's heart
Of prouder stuff than that of Beatrice.
Disdain and scorn ride sparkling in her eyes,   55
Misprizing what they look on; and her wit
Values itself so highly that to her
All matter else seems weak. She cannot love
Nor take no shape nor project of affection,
She is so self-endeared.   60
   Urs.   Sure I think so;
And therefore certainly it were not good
She knew his love, lest she'll make sport at it.
   Hero. Why, you speak truth. I never yet saw man,
How wise, how noble, young, how rarely featured,   65
But she would spell him backward. If fair-faced,
She would swear the gentleman should be her sister;
If black, why, Nature, drawing of an antic,
Made a foul blot; if tall, a lance ill-headed;
If low, an agate very vilely cut;   70
If speaking, why, a vane blown with all winds;
If silent, why, a block moved with none.
So turns she every man the wrong side out
And never gives to truth and virtue that
Which simpleness and merit purchaseth.   75
   Urs. Sure, sure, such carping is not commendable.

77. from all fashions: hard to please; perverse.

89. honest slanders: false accusations that do not touch her honor.

106. every day tomorrow: i.e., tomorrow and every day thereafter.

Hero. No, not to be so odd and from all fashions,
As Beatrice is, cannot be commendable.
But who dare tell her so? If I should speak,
She would mock me into air; O, she would laugh me   80
Out of myself, press me to death with wit!
Therefore let Benedick, like covered fire,
Consume away in sighs, waste inwardly.
It were a better death than die with mocks,
Which is as bad as die with tickling.   85

Urs. Yet tell her of it. Hear what she will say.

Hero. No; rather I will go to Benedick
And counsel him to fight against his passion.
And truly, I'll devise some honest slanders
To stain my cousin with. One doth not know   90
How much an ill word may empoison liking.

Urs. O, do not do your cousin such a wrong!
She cannot be so much without true judgment
(Having so swift and excellent a wit
As she is prized to have) as to refuse   95
So rare a gentleman as Signior Benedick.

Hero. He is the only man of Italy,
Always excepted my dear Claudio.

Urs. I pray you be not angry with me, madam,
Speaking my fancy: Signior Benedick,   100
For shape, for bearing, argument, and valor,
Goes foremost in report through Italy.

Hero. Indeed he hath an excellent good name.

Urs. His excellence did earn it ere he had it.
When are you married, madam?   105

Hero. Why, every day tomorrow! Come, go in.
I'll show thee some attires and have thy counsel

108. **furnish:** outfit.

109. **limed:** caught in the birdlime we have spread.

111. **haps:** chance.

116. **No glory lives behind the back of such:** i.e., nothing favorable is spoken about such qualities behind their backs.

122. **Believe it better than reportingly:** am more firmly convinced of it than mere report could make me.

III. [ii.] Don John sets in motion his plan to disgrace Hero and break off the marriage with Claudio by informing Don Pedro and Claudio that she is faithless, the proof of which they can observe for themselves by watching outside her chamber window that night. Although incredulous that his story can be true, they agree to watch with him.

1–2. **consummate:** consummated.

3. **bring:** accompany.

7–8. **be bold with Benedick for his company:** presume to ask Benedick to accompany me.

Which is the best to furnish me tomorrow.

> [*They walk away.*]

Urs. She's limed, I warrant youl We have caught
her, madam.   110

Hero. If it prove so, then loving goes by haps;
Some Cupid kills with arrows, some with traps.

> *Exeunt* [*Hero and Ursula*].

Beat. What fire is in mine ears? Can this be true?
Stand I condemned for pride and scorn so much?
Contempt, farewelll and maiden pride, adieul   115
No glory lives behind the back of such.
And, Benedick, love on; I will requite thee,
Taming my wild heart to thy loving hand.
If thou dost love, my kindness shall incite thee
To bind our loves up in a holy band;   120
For others say thou dost deserve, and I
Believe it better than reportingly.

> *Exit.*

[Scene II. A room in Leonato's house.]

Enter Don Pedro, Claudio, Benedick, and Leonato.

Pedro. I do but stay till your marriage be consummate, and then go I toward Aragon.

Claud. I'll bring you thither, my lord, if you'll
vouchsafe me.

Pedro. Nay, that would be as great a soil in the new   5
gloss of your marriage as to show a child his new coat
and forbid him to wear it. I will only be bold with

15. **sadder:** graver.

17. **truant:** rogue.

23–4. hang it first and draw it afterwards: traitors were hanged, cut down while still alive, then drawn (disembowelled) and cut into quarters.

26. a humor or a worm: believed to be causes of toothaches. A **humor** is an unhealthy secretion of the body.

30. fancy: love.

34. slops: floppy, full breeches.

37. fool for fancy: slave to amorous inclination.

Dupliciarius miles Germanorum.

German soldier wearing slops. From Pietro Bertelli, *Diversarum nationum habitus* (1594).

Benedick for his company; for, from the crown of his
head to the sole of his foot, he is all mirth. He hath
twice or thrice cut Cupid's bowstring, and the little 10
hangman dare not shoot at him. He hath a heart as
sound as a bell, and his tongue is the clapper, for what
his heart thinks, his tongue speaks.

Bene. Gallants, I am not as I have been.

Leon. So say I. Methinks you are sadder. 15

Claud. I hope he be in love.

Pedro. Hang him, truant! There's no true drop of
blood in him to be truly touched with love. If he be
sad, he wants money.

Bene. I have the toothache. 20

Pedro. Draw it.

Bene. Hang it!

Claud. You must hang it first and draw it afterwards.

Pedro. What? sigh for the toothache? 25

Leon. Where is but a humor or a worm.

Bene. Well, everyone can master a grief but he
that has it.

Claud. Yet say I he is in love.

Pedro. There is no appearance of fancy in him, un- 30
less it be a fancy that he hath to strange disguises;
as to be a Dutchman today, a Frenchman tomorrow;
or in the shape of two countries at once, as a German
from the waist downward, all slops, and a Spaniard
from the hip upward, no doublet. Unless he have a 35
fancy to this foolery, as it appears he hath, he is no
fool for fancy, as you would have it appear he is.

Claud. If he be not in love with some woman, there

44. **tennis balls:** hair was commonly used to stuff tennis balls.

47. **civet:** musk.

51. **note:** sign.

52. **wash his face:** i.e., with cosmetic lotions.

56. **crept into a lutestring:** changed to a plaintive love song; **stops:** (1) frets of a lute; (2) restraints. I.e., his satirical wit is checked by his new emotion.

57. **heavy:** melancholy.

64. **with her face upwards:** i.e., in Benedick's arms.

67–8. **hobbyhorses:** buffoons.

is no believing old signs. 'A brushes his hat o' morn-
ings. What should that bode?   40

Pedro. Hath any man seen him at the barber's?

Claud. No, but the barber's man hath been seen
with him, and the old ornament of his cheek hath
already stuffed tennis balls.

Leon. Indeed he looks younger than he did by the   45
loss of a beard.

Pedro. Nay, 'a rubs himself with civet. Can you
smell him out by that?

Claud. That's as much as to say the sweet youth's
in love.   50

Pedro. The greatest note of it is his melancholy.

Claud. And when was he wont to wash his face?

Pedro. Yea, or to paint himself? for the which I hear
what they say of him.

Claud. Nay, but his jesting spirit, which is now   55
crept into a lutestring and now governed by stops.

Pedro. Indeed that tells a heavy tale for him. Conclude, conclude, he is in love.

Claud. Nay, but I know who loves him.

Pedro. That would I know too. I warrant, one that   60
knows him not.

Claud. Yes, and his ill conditions; and in despite of
all, dies for him.

Pedro. She shall be buried with her face upwards.

Bene. Yet is this no charm for the toothache. Old   65
signior, walk aside with me. I have studied eight or
nine wise words to speak to you, which these hobbyhorses must not hear.

[Exeunt Benedick and Leonato.]

69. **break with him:** inform him.

75. **Good-den:** good evening (afternoon).

89. **aim better at me:** evaluate me more accurately.

90. **holds you well:** thinks highly of you.

95–6. **circumstances short'ned:** abbreviating the details.

Pedro. For my life, to break with him about Bea-
trice!   70

Claud. 'Tis even so. Hero and Margaret have by
this played their parts with Beatrice, and then the
two bears will not bite one another when they meet.

Enter John the Bastard.

John. My lord and brother, God save you.

Pedro. Good-den, brother.   75

John. If your leisure served, I would speak with
you.

Pedro. In private?

John. If it please you. Yet Count Claudio may hear,
for what I would speak of concerns him.   80

Pedro. What's the matter?

John. [*To Claudio*] Means your Lordship to be
married tomorrow?

Pedro. You know he does.

John. I know not that, when he knows what I know.   85

Claudio. If there be any impediment, I pray you
discover it.

John. You may think I love you not. Let that appear
hereafter, and aim better at me by that I now will
manifest. For my brother, I think he holds you well   90
and in dearness of heart hath holp to effect your en-
suing marriage—surely suit ill spent and labor ill bestowed!

Pedro. Why, what's the matter?

John. I came hither to tell you, and, circumstances   95

96. **she has been too long a-talking of:** she is not worth further mention.

102. **paint out:** picture fully.

105. **warrant:** proof.

122. **Bear it coldly:** show no sign of it.

124. **untowardly turned:** turned upside down.

125. **mischief:** misfortune.

short'ned (for she has been too long a-talking of),
the lady is disloyal.

Claud. Who? Hero?

John. Even she—Leonato's Hero, your Hero, every
man's Hero.   100

Claud. Disloyal?

John. The word is too good to paint out her wick-
edness. I could say she were worse; think you of a
worse title and I will fit her to it. Wonder not till further warrant. Go but with me tonight, you shall see   105
her chamber window ent'red, even the night before
her wedding day. If you love her then, tomorrow
wed her; but it would better fit your honor to change
your mind.

Claud. May this be so?   110

Pedro. I will not think it.

John. If you dare not trust that you see, confess not
that you know. If you will follow me, I will show you
enough; and when you have seen more and heard
more, proceed accordingly.   115

Claud. If I see anything tonight why I should not
marry her tomorrow, in the congregation where I
should wed, there will I shame her.

Pedro. And, as I wooed for thee to obtain her, I will
join with thee to disgrace her.   120

John. I will disparage her no farther till you are
my witnesses. Bear it coldly but till midnight and let
the issue show itself.

Pedro. O day untowardly turned!

Claud. O mischief strangely thwarting!   125

126. prevented: avoided.

═══════════════════════════════

III. [iii.] Dogberry, a constable, and his assistant, Verges, assemble the evening's watchmen and give them instructions. The watchmen have not been long at their posts when Borachio and Conrade appear; Borachio is heard to boast drunkenly of the money he has earned from Don John for his night's work of ruining Hero's reputation. Although they imperfectly understand the full meaning of the conversation, the watchmen recognize Borachio as a villain and arrest him and Conrade.

═══════════════════

2. it were pity but they should: it would be a pity if they did not.

3. salvation: i.e., damnation. Shakespeare's comic characters often use big words that mean the opposite of what the sense requires.

14. well-favored: attractive.

John. O plague right well prevented!
So will you say when you have seen the sequel.

Exeunt.

[Scene III. A street.]

*Enter Dogberry and his compartner [Verges],
with the Watch.*

Dog. Are you good men and true?

Verg. Yea, or else it were pity but they should suffer salvation, body and soul.

Dog. Nay, that were a punishment too good for
them, if they should have any allegiance in them, be- 5
ing chosen for the Prince's watch.

Verg. Well, give them their charge, neighbor Dogberry.

Dog. First, who think you the most desartless man
to be constable? 10

1. Watch. Hugh Oatcake, sir, or George Seacoal;
for they can write and read.

Dog. Come hither, neighbor Seacoal. God hath
blessed you with a good name. To be a well-favored
man is the gift of Fortune, but to write and read 15
comes by Nature.

2. Watch. Both which, Master Constable—

Dog. You have. I knew it would be your answer.
Well, for your favor, sir, why, give God thanks and
make no boast of it; and for your writing and read- 20

25. **vagrom:** vagrant.
41. **bills:** long-handled weapons, carried by soldiers and watchmen.
50. **true:** honest.

ing, let that appear when there is no need of such
vanity. You are thought here to be the most senseless
and fit man for the constable of the watch. Therefore
bear you the lantern. This is your charge: you shall
comprehend all vagrom men; you are to bid any man   25
stand, in the Prince's name.

2. Watch. How if 'a will not stand?

Dog. Why then, take no note of him but let him go,
and presently call the rest of the watch together and
thank God you are rid of a knave.   30

Verg. If he will not stand when he is bidden, he
is none of the Prince's subjects.

Dog. True, and they are to meddle with none but
the Prince's subjects. You shall also make no noise in
the streets; for for the watch to babble and to talk is   35
most tolerable and not to be endured.

2. Watch. We will rather sleep than talk. We know
what belongs to a watch.

Dog. Why, you speak like an ancient and most quiet
watchman, for I cannot see how sleeping should of-   40
fend. Only have a care that your bills be not stol'n.
Well, you are to call at all the alehouses and bid those
that are drunk get them to bed.

2. Watch. How if they will not?

Dog. Why then, let them alone till they are sober.   45
If they make you not then the better answer, you
may say they are not the men you took them for.

2. Watch. Well, sir.

Dog. If you meet a thief, you may suspect him, by
virtue of your office, to be no true man; and for such   50

74. **present**: represent.

kind of men, the less you meddle or make with them,
why, the more is for your honesty.

2. Watch. If we know him to be a thief, shall we
not lay hands on him?

Dog. Truly, by your office you may; but I think 55
they that touch pitch will be defiled. The most peace-
able way for you, if you do take a thief, is to let him
show himself what he is and steal out of your company.

Verg. You have been always called a merciful man, 60
partner.

Dog. Truly, I would not hang a dog by my will,
much more a man who hath any honesty in him.

Verg. If you hear a child cry in the night, you must
call to the nurse and bid her still it. 65

2. Watch. How if the nurse be asleep and will not
hear us?

Dog. Why then, depart in peace and let the child
wake her with crying; for the ewe that will not hear
her lamb when it baes will never answer a calf when 70
he bleats.

Verg. 'Tis very true.

Dog. This is the end of the charge: you, constable,
are to present the Prince's own person. If you meet
the Prince in the night, you may stay him. 75

Verg. Nay, by'r lady, that I think 'a cannot.

Dog. Five shillings to one on't with any man that
knows the statutes, he may stay him! Marry, not without the Prince be willing; for indeed the watch ought
to offend no man, and it is an offense to stay a man 80
against his will.

99. **scab:** secondary meaning "rogue."

102. **penthouse:** sloping roof.

103. **like a true drunkard:** the Spanish word *borracho* means "drunkard."

Verg. By'r lady, I think it be so.

Dog. Ha, ah, ha! Well, masters, good night. And
there be any matter of weight chances, call up me.
Keep your fellows' counsels and your own, and good   85
night. Come, neighbor.

2. Watch. Well, masters, we hear our charge. Let
us go sit here upon the church bench till two, and
then all to bed.

Dog. One word more, honest neighbors. I pray you   90
watch about Signior Leonato's door; for the wedding
being there tomorrow, there is a great coil tonight.
Adieu. Be vigitant, I beseech you.

                    Exeunt [Dogberry and Verges].

                Enter Borachio and Conrade.

Bora. What, Conrade!

2. Watch. [*Aside*] Peace! stir not!   95

Bora. Conrade, I say!

Con. Here, man. I am at thy elbow.

Bora. Mass, and my elbow itched! I thought there
would a scab follow.

Con. I will owe thee an answer for that; and now   100
forward with thy tale.

Bora. Stand thee close, then, under this penthouse,
for it drizzles rain, and I will, like a true drunkard,
utter all to thee.

2. Watch. [*Aside*] Some treason, masters. Yet stand   105
close.

Bora. Therefore know I have earned of Don John
a thousand ducats.

116. **unconfirmed:** inexperienced.
123. **deformed:** deforming.
134. **reechy:** grimy.

Con. Is it possible that any villainy should be so dear? 110

Bora. Thou shouldst rather ask if it were possible any villainy should be so rich; for when rich villains have need of poor ones, poor ones may make what price they will.

Con. I wonder at it. 115

Bora. That shows thou art unconfirmed. Thou knowest that the fashion of a doublet, or a hat, or a cloak, is nothing to a man.

Con. Yes, it is apparel.

Bora. I mean the fashion. 120

Con. Yes, the fashion is the fashion.

Bora. Tush! I may as well say the fool's the fool. But seest thou not what a deformed thief this fashion is?

2. Watch. [*Aside*] I know that Deformed. 'A has 125 been a vile thief this seven year; 'a goes up and down like a gentleman. I remember his name.

Bora. Didst thou not hear somebody?

Con. No; 'twas the vane on the house.

Bora. Seest thou not, I say, what a deformed thief 130 this fashion is? how giddily 'a turns about all the hot-bloods between fourteen and five-and-thirty? sometimes fashioning them like Pharaoh's soldiers in the reechy painting, sometime like god Bel's priests in the old church window, sometime like the shaven 135 Hercules in the smirched, worm-eaten tapestry, where his codpiece seems as massy as his club?

Con. All this I see; and I see that the fashion wears out more apparel than the man. But art not thou thy-

148. **possessed:** governed (as though Don John were a demon).

149. **amiable:** loving.

153. **possessed:** convinced.

157. **appointed:** engaged.

164. **recovered:** discovered or uncovered.

165. **lechery:** villainy.

167. **a lock:** a long lock of hair by one ear, such as was affected by gentlemen.

self giddy with the fashion too, that thou hast shifted 140
out of thy tale into telling me of the fashion?

Bora. Not so neither. But know that I have tonight
wooed Margaret, the Lady Hero's gentlewoman, by
the name of Hero. She leans me out at her mistress'
chamber window, bids me a thousand times good 145
night—I tell this tale vilely; I should first tell thee
how the Prince, Claudio, and my master, planted and
placed and possessed by my master Don John, saw
afar off in the orchard this amiable encounter.

Con. And thought they Margaret was Hero? 150

Bora. Two of them did, the Prince and Claudio;
but the devil my master knew she was Margaret; and
partly by his oaths, which first possessed them, partly
by the dark night, which did deceive them, but chiefly
by my villainy, which did confirm any slander that 155
Don John had made, away went Claudio enraged;
swore he would meet her, as he was appointed, next
morning at the temple and there, before the whole
congregation, shame her with what he saw o'ernight
and send her home again without a husband. 160

1. Watch. We charge you in the Prince's name
stand!

2. Watch. Call up the right Master Constable. We
have here recovered the most dangerous piece of
lechery that ever was known in the commonwealth. 165

1. Watch. And one Deformed is one of them. I
know him; 'a wears a lock.

Con. Masters, masters—

2. Watch. You'll be made bring Deformed forth, I
warrant you. 170

172. **obey:** persuade, induce, or the like.

174. **like:** likely; **a goodly commodity:** profitable merchandise.

175. **of these men's bills:** (1) on the credit of these men; (2) with the weapons of these men.

176. **in question:** (1) questionable; (2) subject to question.

III. [iv.] The innocent Hero prepares for her wedding. While she dresses, she and Margaret tease Beatrice about their suspicion that she is in love with Benedick. Beatrice is so altered that she seems unable to jest with her usual sharpness.

6. **rebato:** a stiff collar that stood out around the neck.

12. **tire:** headdress; **within:** in the other room.

12–3. **the hair:** apparently the headdress included a wig, as was common in elaborate formal coiffures.

Con. Masters—

1. Watch. Never speak, we charge you. Let us obey you to go with us.

Bora. We are like to prove a goodly commodity, being taken up of these men's bills.   175

Con. A commodity in question, I warrant you. Come, we'll obey you.

                                             Exeunt.

[Scene IV. Hero's apartment.]

Enter Hero, Margaret, and Ursula.

Hero. Good Ursula, wake my cousin Beatrice and desire her to rise.

Urs. I will, lady.

Hero. And bid her come hither.

Urs. Well.   [*Exit.*]   5

Marg. Troth, I think your other rebato were better.

Hero. No, pray thee, good Meg, I'll wear this.

Marg. By my troth, 's not so good, and I warrant your cousin will say so.

Hero. My cousin 's a fool, and thou art another. I'll   10
wear none but this.   ·

Marg. I like the new tire within excellently, if the hair were a thought browner; and your gown 's a most rare fashion, i' faith. I saw the Duchess of Milan's gown that they praise so.   15

Hero. O, that exceeds, they say.

17–8. **nightgown:** dressing gown, negligee; **in respect of:** compared with.

18. **cuts:** decorative slashes.

19. **down sleeves:** long sleeves; **side-sleeves:** sleeves that did not enclose the arm but hung behind or alongside the other sleeve in an ornamental manner.

20. **round underborne:** stiffened underneath at the bottom.

21. **quaint:** elegant.

31. **saving your reverence:** an apology for an allusion that might offend.

32. **wrest:** distort.

35. **light:** unchaste.

42. **Clap's into:** give us a lively rendition of.

43. **burden:** under-refrain, with a pun referring back to her comment in lines 25–6.

44. **"Light-o'-love" with your heels:** wanton one.

A Milanese woman. From Pietro Bertelli, *Diversarum nationum habitus* (1594).

57

Marg. By my troth, 's but a nightgown in respect
of yours—cloth o' gold and cuts, and laced with silver, set with pearls, down sleeves, side-sleeves, and
skirts, round underborne with a bluish tinsel. But for   20
a fine, quaint, graceful, and excellent fashion, yours
is worth ten on't.

Hero. God give me joy to wear it! for my heart is
exceeding heavy.

Marg. 'Twill be heavier soon by the weight of a   25
man.

Hero. Fie upon thee! art not ashamed?

Marg. Of what, lady? of speaking honorably? Is not
marriage honorable in a beggar? Is not your lord honorable without marriage? I think you would have me   30
say, saving your reverence, "a husband." And bad
thinking do not wrest true speaking, I'll offend nobody. Is there any harm in "the heavier for a husband"? None, I think, and it be the right husband
and the right wife. Otherwise 'tis light, and not heavy.   35
Ask my Lady Beatrice else. Here she comes.

Enter Beatrice.

Hero. Good morrow, coz.

Beat. Good morrow, sweet Hero.

Hero. Why, how now? Do you speak in the sick
tune?   40

Beat. I am out of all other tune, methinks.

Marg. Clap's into "Light-o'-love." That goes without a burden. Do you sing it, and I'll dance it.

Beat. Yea, "Light-o'-love" with your heels! then, if

47. **construction:** interpretation.

53. **For:** because of; **H:** i.e., ache (pronounced like the letter H).

54. **be not turned Turk:** have not renounced your former faith (her determination to have nothing to do with love).

55. **star:** North Star.

56. **trow:** trow you; do you suppose.

65. **professed apprehension:** made a claim to be witty.

70–1. **Carduus benedictus:** blessed thistle, a plant considered curative of many ills of mind and body.

72. **qualm:** spell of illness.

your husband have stables enough, you'll see he shall   45
lack no barns.

Marg. O illegitimate construction! I scorn that with
my heels.

Beat. 'Tis almost five o'clock, cousin; 'tis time you
were ready. By my troth, I am exceeding ill. Heigh-   50
ho!

Marg. For a hawk, a horse, or a husband?

Beat. For the letter that begins them all, H.

Marg. Well, and you be not turned Turk, there's no
more sailing by the star.   55

Beat. What means the fool, trow?

Marg. Nothing I; but God send everyone their
heart's desire!

Hero. These gloves the Count sent me; they are an
excellent perfume.   60

Beat. I am stuffed, cousin; I cannot smell.

Marg. A maid, and stuffed! There's goodly catching
of cold.

Beat. O, God help me! God help me! How long
have you professed apprehension?   65

Marg. Ever since you left it. Doth not my wit become me rarely?

Beat. It is not seen enough. You should wear it in
your cap. By my troth, I am sick.

Marg. Get you some of this distilled *Carduus bene-*   70
dictus and lay it to your heart. It is the only thing for
a qualm.

Hero. There thou prickst her with a thistle.

Beat. Benedictus? why *benedictus?* You have some
moral in this *benedictus.*   75

79–80. **what I list:** what pleases me; **nor I list not to think what I can:** nor do I wish to think what I must (regarding Beatrice's resistance to love).

85–6. **eats his meat without grudging:** i.e., has to admit that he has an appetite like any other man.

90. **false gallop:** literally a horse's canter. Margaret means that her tongue is on the right track.

III. [v.] Dogberry and Verges, attempting to inform Leonato of the two rogues that they have apprehended, are so slow in coming to the point that Leonato impatiently requests that they examine the men and bring the information to him later.

Ent. Headborough: the title of a local constable.

Marg. Moral? No, by my troth, I have no moral
meaning; I meant plain holy thistle. You may think
perchance that I think you are in love. Nay, by'r Lady,
I am not such a fool to think what I list; nor I list not
to think what I can; nor indeed I cannot think, if I   80
would think my heart out of thinking, that you are in
love, or that you will be in love, or that you can be
in love. Yet Benedick was such another, and now is
he become a man. He swore he would never marry;
and yet now in despite of his heart he eats his meat   85
without grudging; and how you may be converted I
know not, but methinks you look with your eyes as
other women do.

Beat. What pace is this that thy tongue keeps?

Marg. Not a false gallop.   90

Enter Ursula.

Urs. Madam, withdraw. The Prince, the Count,
Signior Benedick, Don John, and all the gallants of
the town are come to fetch you to church.

Hero. Help to dress me, good coz, good Meg, good
Ursula.   95

[*Exeunt.*]

[Scene V. The hall in Leonato's house.]

Enter Leonato, and the Constable [*Dogberry*],
and the Headborough [*Verges*].

Leon. What would you with me, honest neighbor?

2. **confidence:** conference.

3. **nearly:** closely.

12. **honest as the skin between his brows:** a proverbial idea.

15. **Comparisons are odorous:** a distortion of the old proverb "Comparisons are odious"; **Palabras:** *pocas palabras* (Spanish for "few words").

24. **exclamation on:** acclamation of.

29–30. **excepting your Worship's presence:** if your Honor will excuse my saying so. As Verges uses this conventional phrase, it gives the implication that "His Worship" is perhaps a more complete knave than the two taken by the watch.

30. **arrant:** out-and-out.

Dog. Marry, sir, I would have some confidence with you that decerns you nearly.

Leon. Brief, I pray you; for you see it is a busy time with me.　　　　　5

Dog. Marry, this it is, sir.

Verg. Yes, in truth it is, sir.

Leon. What is it, my good friends?

Dog. Goodman Verges, sir, speaks a little off the matter—an old man, sir, and his wits are not so blunt　10 as, God help, I would desire they were; but, in faith, honest as the skin between his brows.

Verg. Yes, I thank God I am as honest as any man living that is an old man and no honester than I.

Dog. Comparisons are odorous. *Palabras,* neighbor　15 Verges.

Leon. Neighbors, you are tedious.

Dog. It pleases your Worship to say so, but we are the poor Duke's officers; but truly, for mine own part, if I were as tedious as a king, I could find in my heart　20 to bestow it all of your Worship.

Leon. All thy tediousness on me, ah?

Dog. Yea, and 'twere a thousand pound more than 'tis; for I hear as good exclamation on your Worship as of any man in the city; and though I be but a poor　25 man, I am glad to hear it.

Verg. And so am I.

Leon. I would fain know what you have to say.

Verg. Marry, sir, our watch tonight, excepting your Worship's presence, ha' ta'en a couple of as arrant　30 knaves as any in Messina.

Dog. A good old man, sir; he will be talking. As

34. **a world to see:** a wonder to behold.
36. **ride behind:** i.e., be inferior in intellect.
44. **aspicious:** suspicious.
50. **suffigance:** sufficient.

they say, "When the age is in, the wit is out." God
help us! it is a world to see! Well said, i' faith, neighbor Verges. Well, God's a good man. And two men   35
ride of a horse, one must ride behind. An honest soul,
i' faith, sir, by my troth he is, as ever broke bread; but
God is to be worshiped; all men are not alike, alas,
good neighbor!

Leon. Indeed, neighbor, he comes too short of you.   40

Dog. Gifts that God gives.

Leon. I must leave you.

Dog. One word, sir. Our watch, sir, have indeed
comprehended two aspicious persons, and we would
have them this morning examined before your Wor-   45
ship.

Leon. Take their examination yourself and bring it
me. I am now in great haste, as it may appear unto
you.

Dog. It shall be suffigance.   50

Leon. Drink some wine ere you go. Fare you well.

[*Enter a Messenger.*]

Mess. My lord, they stay for you to give your daughter to her husband.

Leon. I'll wait upon them: I am ready.

                [*Exeunt Leonato and Messenger.*]

Dog. Go, good partner, go get you to Francis Sea-   55
coal; bid him bring his pen and inkhorn to the jail.
We are now to examination these men.

Verg. And we must do it wisely.

60. **non-come:** Dogberry probably confuses "non-plus" with *non compos mentis* (of unsound mind).
61–2. **excommunication:** communication.

Dog. We will spare for no wit, I warrant you. Here's that shall drive some of them to a non-come. Only 60 get the learned writer to set down our excommunication, and meet me at the jail.

            Exeunt.

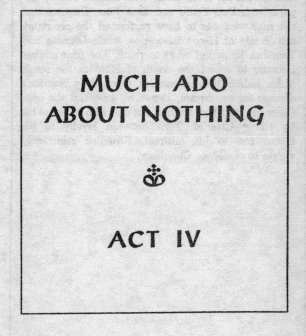

MUCH ADO
ABOUT NOTHING

❦

ACT IV

IV. [i.] The company assembles for the marriage of Claudio and Hero. When Hero's hand is given to him, Claudio charges her with unchastity and Don Pedro confirms the midnight rendezvous they both had witnessed. Hero faints and Claudio hastily departs with Don Pedro and Don John. Beatrice and the friar who was to have performed the ceremony are certain of Hero's innocence, while Leonato and Benedick know not what to think. The friar advises Leonato to report the death of Hero as the result of her public shame. Benedick, touched by Beatrice's distress for her cousin, avows his love and she confesses her own love for him but asks him to prove his by killing Claudio. Torn between loyalty to his friend and to his mistress, Benedick reluctantly agrees to challenge Claudio.

ACT IV

[Scene I. A church.]

Enter Don Pedro, [John the] Bastard, Leonato, Friar,
Claudio, Benedick, Hero, Beatrice, [and Attendants].

Leon. Come, Friar Francis, be brief. Only to the
plain form of marriage, and you shall recount their
particular duties afterwards.

Friar. You come hither, my lord, to marry this lady?

Claud. No.   5

Leon. To be married to her, Friar; you come to
marry her.

Friar. Lady, you come hither to be married to this
count?

Hero. I do.   10

Friar. If either of you know any inward impediment why you should not be conjoined, I charge you
on your souls to utter it.

Claud. Know you any, Hero?

Hero. None, my lord.   15

Friar. Know you any, Count?

Leon. I dare make his answer—none.

Claud. O, what men dare do! what men may do!
what men daily do, not knowing what they do!

63

20. **interjections:** what follows is a quotation from a standard school text of the period, William Lily's Latin grammar.

30. **learn:** teach.

36. **authority and show:** convincing appearance.

38. **blood:** blush.

42. **luxurious:** lustful.

46. **approved:** proven.

47. **proof:** trial.

Bene. How now? interjections? Why then, some be 20
of laughing, as, ah, ha, he!

Claud. Stand thee by, Friar. Father, by your leave:
Will you with free and unconstrained soul
Give me this maid your daughter?

Leon. As freely, son, as God did give her me. 25

Claud. And what have I to give you back whose
worth
May counterpoise this rich and precious gift?

Pedro. Nothing, unless you render her again.

Claud. Sweet Prince, you learn me noble thank- 30
fulness.
There, Leonato, take her back again.
Give not this rotten orange to your friend:
She's but the sign and semblance of her honor.
Behold how like a maid she blushes here! 35
O, what authority and show of truth
Can cunning sin cover itself withal!
Comes not that blood as modest evidence
To witness simple virtue? Would you not swear,
All you that see her, that she were a maid 40
By these exterior shows? But she is none:
She knows the heat of a luxurious bed;
Her blush is guiltiness, not modesty.

Leon. What do you mean, my lord?

Claud. Not to be married, 45
Not to knit my soul to an approved wanton.

Leon. Dear my lord, if you, in your own proof,
Have vanquished the resistance of her youth
And made defeat of her virginity—

60. **Dian:** the moon-goddess Diana.

61. **blown:** in full bloom.

65. **wide:** wide of the mark and beyond the bounds of decorum.

Diana, the moon-goddess. From Vincenzo Cartari, *Imagini de gli dei delli antichi* (1615).

Claud. I know what you would say. If I have   50
    known her,
You will say she did embrace me as a husband,
And so extenuate the forehand sin.
No, Leonato,
I never tempted her with word too large   55
But as a brother to his sister showed
Bashful sincerity and comely love.
    Hero. And seemed I ever otherwise to you?
    Claud. Out on the seeming! I will write against it.
You seem to me as Dian in her orb,   60
As chaste as is the bud ere it be blown,
But you are more intemperate in your blood
Than Venus or those pamp'red animals
That rage in savage sensuality.
    Hero. Is my lord well that he doth speak so wide?   65
    Leon. Sweet Prince, why speak not you?
    Pedro.   What should I speak?
I stand dishonored that have gone about
To link my dear friend to a common stale.
    Leon. Are these things spoken, or do I but dream?   70
    John. Sir, they are spoken, and these things are
    true.
    Bene. This looks not like a nuptial.
    Hero.   "True!" O God!
    Claud. Leonato, stand I here?   75
Is this the Prince? Is this the Prince's brother?
Is this face Hero's? Are our eyes our own?
    Leon. All this is so; but what of this, my lord?
    Claud. Let me but move one question to your
    daughter,   80

81. fatherly and kindly power: i.e., the power of her natural father.

86. your name: i.e., the name that you deserve.

90. Hero itself: i.e., the utterance of the name Hero by the man at her window.

97. grieved: wronged.

100. liberal: licentious.

And, by that fatherly and kindly power
That you have in her, bid her answer truly.

   Leon. I charge thee do so, as thou art my child.

   Hero. O, God defend me! How am I beset!
What kind of catechizing call you this?   85

   Claud. To make you answer truly to your name.

   Hero. Is it not Hero? Who can blot that name
With any just reproach?

   Claud.   Marry, that can Hero!
Hero itself can blot out Hero's virtue.   90
What man was he talked with you yesternight,
Out at your window betwixt twelve and one?
Now, if you are a maid, answer to this.

   Hero. I talked with no man at that hour, my lord.

   Pedro. Why, then are you no maiden. Leonato,   95
I am sorry you must hear. Upon my honor,
Myself, my brother, and this grieved Count
Did see her, hear her, at that hour last night
Talk with a ruffian at her chamber window,
Who hath indeed, most like a liberal villain,   100
Confessed the vile encounters they have had
A thousand times in secret.

   John. Fie, fie! they are not to be named, my lord—
Not to be spoke of;
There is not chastity enough in language   105
Without offense to utter them. Thus, pretty lady,
I am sorry for thy much misgovernment.

   Claud. O Hero! what a Hero hadst thou been
If half thy outward graces had been placed
About thy thoughts and counsels of thy heart!   110

114. **conjecture:** suspicion.
115. **thoughts of harm:** condemnations.
116. **gracious:** virtuous.
139. **spirits:** animal spirits; **shames:** sense of shame.

But fare thee well, most foul, most fair! Farewell,
Thou pure impiety and impious purity!
For thee I'll lock up all the gates of love,
And on my eyelids shall conjecture hang,
To turn all beauty into thoughts of harm,   115
And never shall it more be gracious.

     Leon. Hath no man's dagger here a point for me?
                         [*Hero swoons.*]

     Beat. Why, how now, cousin? Wherefore sink you
     down?

     John. Come, let us go. These things, come thus to   120
     light,
Smother her spirits up.
        [*Exeunt Don Pedro, Don John, and Claudio.*]

     Bene. How doth the lady?

     Beat.   Dead, I think. Help, uncle!
Hero! why, Hero! Uncle! Signior Benedick! Friar!   125

     Leon. O Fate, take not away thy heavy hand!
Death is the fairest cover for her shame
That may be wished for.

     Beat.   How now, cousin Hero?

     Friar. Have comfort, lady.   130

     Leon. Dost thou look up?

     Friar.   Yea, wherefore should she not?

     Leon. Wherefore? Why, doth not every earthly
     thing
Cry shame upon her? Could she here deny   135
The story that is printed in her blood?
Do not live, Hero; do not ope thine eyes;
For, did I think thou wouldst not quickly die,
Thought I thy spirits were stronger than thy shames,

140. **on the rearward of reproaches:** after reproaching you.

142. **frame:** plan.

146. **issue:** offspring.

152–53. **I myself was to myself not mine,/Valuing of her:** I loved her more than I loved myself.

156. **season:** preservation.

Myself would on the rearward of reproaches   140
Strike at thy life. Grieved I, I had but one?
Chid I for that at frugal Nature's frame?
O, one too much by thee! Why had I one?
Why ever wast thou lovely in my eyes?
Why had I not with charitable hand   145
Took up a beggar's issue at my gates,
Who smirched thus and mired with infamy,
I might have said, "No part of it is mine;
This shame derives itself from unknown loins"?
But mine, and mine I loved, and mine I praised,   150
And mine that I was proud on—mine so much
That I myself was to myself not mine,
Valuing of her—why, she, O, she is fall'n
Into a pit of ink, that the wide sea
Hath drops too few to wash her clean again   155
And salt too little which may season give
To her foul tainted flesh!

   Bene.   Sir, sir, be patient.
For my part, I am so attired in wonder,
I know not what to say.   160

   Beat. O, on my soul, my cousin is belied!

   Bene. Lady, were you her bedfellow last night?

   Beat. No, truly, not; although, until last night,
I have this twelvemonth been her bedfellow.

   Leon. Confirmed, confirmed! O, that is stronger   165
     made
Which was before barred up with ribs of iron!
Would the two princes lie? and Claudio lie,
Who loved her so that, speaking of her foulness,
Washed it with tears? Hence from her! let her die.   170

175. **blushing apparitions:** shows of blushing.

179. **errors:** i.e., opinions that are false to the point of heresy.

181. **reading:** interpretation.

182–83. **Which with experimental seal doth warrant/The tenor of my book:** which has the seal of experience to confirm that my reading of her face is correct.

184. **reverence:** my profession, which merits respect; **divinity:** knowledge of theology.

192. **proper nakedness:** i.e., a nakedness which she has done nothing to clothe.

198. **Prove you:** if you can prove that.

199. **unmeet:** improper.

201. **Refuse:** reject.

Friar. Hear me a little;
For I have only been silent so long,
And given way unto this course of fortune,
By noting of the lady. I have marked
A thousand blushing apparitions   175
To start into her face, a thousand innocent shames
In angel whiteness beat away those blushes,
And in her eye there hath appeared a fire
To burn the errors that these princes hold
Against her maiden truth. Call me a fool;   180
Trust not my reading nor my observations,
Which with experimental seal doth warrant
The tenor of my book; trust not my age,
My reverence, calling, nor divinity,
If this sweet lady lie not guiltless here   185
Under some biting error.
   Leon.   Friar, it cannot be.
Thou seest that all the grace that she hath left
Is that she will not add to her damnation
A sin of perjury: she not denies it.   190
Why seekst thou, then, to cover with excuse
That which appears in proper nakedness?
   Friar. Lady, what man is he you are accused of?
   Hero. They know that do accuse me; I know none.
If I know more of any man alive   195
Than that which maiden modesty doth warrant,
Let all my sins lack mercy! O my father,
Prove you that any man with me conversed
At hours unmeet, or that I yesternight
Maintained the change of words with any creature,   200
Refuse me, hate me, torture me to death!

202. **misprision:** mistake.

204. **have the very bent of honor:** are fashioned in honor's very image; are honorable through and through.

206. **practice:** plot.

207. **frame:** fashioning.

215. **in such a kind:** to such a degree.

218. **quit me of them throughly:** repay them thoroughly.

224. **mourning ostentation:** show of mourning.

228. **become of this:** be the consequence of this.

231. **remorse:** compassion.

Friar. There is some strange misprision in the
    princes.
    Bene. Two of them have the very bent of honor;
And if their wisdoms be misled in this,   205
The practice of it lives in John the Bastard,
Whose spirits toil in frame of villainies.
    Leon. I know not. If they speak but truth of her,
These hands shall tear her. If they wrong her honor,
The proudest of them shall well hear of it.   210
Time hath not yet so dried this blood of mine,
Nor age so eat up my invention,
Nor fortune made such havoc of my means,
Nor my bad life reft me so much of friends,
But they shall find awaked in such a kind   215
Both strength of limb and policy of mind,
Ability in means, and choice of friends,
To quit me of them throughly.
    Friar.   Pause awhile
And let my counsel sway you in this case.   220
Your daughter here the princes left for dead,
Let her awhile be secretly kept in
And publish it that she is dead indeed;
Maintain a mourning ostentation,
And on your family's old monument   225
Hang mournful epitaphs and do all rites
That appertain unto a burial.
    Leon. What shall become of this? What will this
    do?
    Friar. Marry, this well carried shall on her behalf 230
Change slander to remorse. That is some good.

240. rack: stretch.

244. idea: image; **her life:** herself when alive.

245. study of imagination: reflection; meditation.

247. habit: attire.

251. had interest in: owned a part of; **liver:** (considered the seat of passion).

255. event: result.

257. aim: supposition; **leveled false:** aimed inaccurately; erroneous.

260. sort: turn out.

But not for that dream I on this strange course,
But on this travail look for greater birth.
She dying, as it must be so maintained,
Upon the instant that she was accused,   235
Shall be lamented, pitied, and excused
Of every hearer; for it so falls out
That what we have we prize not to the worth
Whiles we enjoy it, but being lacked and lost,
Why, then we rack the value, then we find   240
The virtue that possession would not show us
Whiles it was ours. So will it fare with Claudio.
When he shall hear she died upon his words,
The idea of her life shall sweetly creep
Into his study of imagination,   245
And every lovely organ of her life
Shall come appareled in more precious habit,
More moving, delicate, and full of life,
Into the eye and prospect of his soul
Than when she lived indeed. Then shall he mourn 250
(If ever love had interest in his liver)
And wish he had not so accused her—
No, though he thought his accusation true.
Let this be so, and doubt not but success
Will fashion the event in better shape   255
Than I can lay it down in likelihood.
But if all aim but this be leveled false,
The supposition of the lady's death
Will quench the wonder of her infamy.
And if it sort not well, you may conceal her,   260
As best befits her wounded reputation,

265. **inwardness and love:** deep affection.

270. **flow in grief:** drift in tears; am mastered by sorrow.

273. **to strange sores strangely they strain the cure:** proverbial, "Desperate cuts must have desperate cures."

275. **prolonged:** postponed.

279. **You have no reason. I do it freely:** i.e., there is no need for you to ask me to weep, since I do it willingly.

285. **even:** smooth; easy.

In some reclusive and religious life,
Out of all eyes, tongues, minds, and injuries.

Bene. Signior Leonato, let the friar advise you;
And though you know my inwardness and love   265
Is very much unto the Prince and Claudio,
Yet, by mine honor, I will deal in this
As secretly and justly as your soul
Should with your body.

Leon.   Being that I flow in grief,   270
The smallest twine may lead me.

Friar. 'Tis well consented. Presently away;
For to strange sores strangely they strain the cure.
Come, lady, die to live. This wedding day
Perhaps is but prolonged. Have patience and endure. 275

            Exeunt [all but Benedick and Beatrice].

Bene. Lady Beatrice, have you wept all this while?

Beat. Yea, and I will weep a while longer.

Bene. I will not desire that.

Beat. You have no reason. I do it freely.

Bene. Surely I do believe your fair cousin is 280
wronged.

Beat. Ah, how much might the man deserve of me
that would right her!

Bene. Is there any way to show such friendship?

Beat. A very even way, but no such friend.   285

Bene. May a man do it?

Beat. It is a man's office, but not yours.

Bene. I do love nothing in the world so well as you.
Is not that strange?

Beat. As strange as the thing I know not. It were 290
as possible for me to say I loved nothing so well as

295. Do not swear, and eat it: do not swear your love for fear you may be forced to eat your words.

297. eat it: eat my sword.

303. happy: opportune.

321. in the height: in the highest degree.

you. But believe me not; and yet I lie not. I confess
nothing, nor I deny nothing. I am sorry for my cousin.

Bene. By my sword, Beatrice, thou lovest me.

Beat. Do not swear, and eat it.   295

Bene. I will swear by it that you love me, and I will
make him eat it that says I love not you.

Beat. Will you not eat your word?

Bene. With no sauce that can be devised to it. I
protest I love thee.   300

Beat. Why then, God forgive me!

Bene. What offense, sweet Beatrice?

Beat. You have stayed me in a happy hour. I was
about to protest I loved you.

Bene. And do it with all thy heart.   305

Beat. I love you with so much of my heart that
none is left to protest.

Bene. Come, bid me do anything for thee.

Beat. Kill Claudio.

Bene. Ha! not for the wide world!   310

Beat. You kill me to deny it. Farewell.

Bene. Tarry, sweet Beatrice.

Beat. I am gone, though I am here. There is no love
in you. Nay, I pray you let me go.

Bene. Beatrice—   315

Beat. In faith, I will go.

Bene. We'll be friends first.

Beat. You dare easier be friends with me than fight
with mine enemy.

Bene. Is Claudio thine enemy?   320

Beat. Is 'a not approved in the height a villain, that
hath slandered, scorned, dishonored my kinswoman?

323. **bear her in hand:** "string her along."
325. **uncovered:** unconcealed.
329. **proper:** fine (ironic).
336. **goodly count:** (1) handsome count; (2) fine tale; **Comfect:** confection.
339. **compliment:** politeness.
340. **trim:** splendid (ironic).

O that I were a man! What? bear her in hand until
they come to take hands, and then with public
accusation, uncovered slander, unmitigated rancor— 325
O God, that I were a man! I would eat his heart in the
market place.

Bene. Hear me, Beatrice!

Beat. Talk with a man out at a window!—a proper
saying! 330

Bene. Nay, but Beatrice—

Beat. Sweet Hero! She is wronged, she is sland'red,
she is undone.

Bene. Beat—

Beat. Princes and Counties! Surely a princely testi- 335
mony, a goodly count, Count Comfect, a sweet gallant
surely! O that I were a man for his sake! or that I had
any friend would be a man for my sake! But manhood
is melted into curtsies, valor into compliment, and
men are only turned into tongue, and trim ones too. 340
He is now as valiant as Hercules that only tells a lie
and swears it. I cannot be a man with wishing; therefore I will die a woman with grieving.

Bene. Tarry, good Beatrice. By this hand, I love
thee. 345

Beat. Use it for my love some other way than
swearing by it.

Bene. Think you in your soul the Count Claudio
hath wronged Hero?

Beat. Yea, as sure as I have a thought or a soul. 350

Bene. Enough, I am engaged; I will challenge him.
I will kiss your hand, and so I leave you. By this
hand, Claudio shall render me a dear account. As you

IV. [ii.] Dogberry and Verges are informed by the watch of the villainy disclosed by Borachio and face the two prisoners. The news that Don John has secretly left Messina and that Hero is dead as the result of Claudio's repudiation seems to confirm the truth of Borachio's story. Dogberry orders the two men to be fettered and taken before Leonato.

〜〜〜〜〜〜〜〜〜〜〜〜〜〜〜〜

5. exhibition: Dogberry's malapropism for "commission."

hear of me, so think of me. Go comfort your cousin.
I must say she is dead—and so farewell.   355

[*Exeunt.*]

<hr />

[Scene II. A prison.]

*Enter the Constables [Dogberry and Verges] and the
Sexton, in gowns, [and the Watch, with Conrade and]
Borachio.*

Dog. Is our whole dissembly appeared?

Verg. O, a stool and a cushion for the sexton.

Sex. Which be the malefactors?

Dog. Marry, that am I and my partner.

Verg. Nay, that's certain. We have the exhibition to   5
examine.

Sex. But which are the offenders that are to be examined? Let them come before Master Constable.

Dog. Yea, marry, let them come before me. What
is your name, friend?   10

Bora. Borachio.

Dog. Pray write down Borachio. Yours, sirrah?

Con. I am a gentleman, sir, and my name is
Conrade.

Dog. Write down Master Gentleman Conrade.   15
Masters, do you serve God?

Both. Yea, sir, we hope.

Dog. Write down that they hope they serve God;
and write God first, for God defend but God should
go before such villains! Masters, it is proved already   20

26. go about with: handle; deal with.
30–1. in a tale: i.e., their stories agree.
35. eftest: probably, "aptest."

that you are little better than false knaves, and it will
go near to be thought so shortly. How answer you for
yourselves?

Con. Marry, sir, we say we are none.

Dog. A marvelous witty fellow, I assure you; but I   25
will go about with him. Come you hither, sirrah. A
word in your ear. Sir, I say to you, it is thought you
are false knaves.

Bora. Sir, I say to you we are none.

Dog. Well, stand aside. Fore God, they are both in   30
a tale. Have you writ down that they are none?

Sex. Master Constable, you go not the way to examine. You must call forth the watch that are their
accusers.

Dog. Yea, marry, that's the eftest way. Let the   35
watch come forth. Masters, I charge you in the
Prince's name accuse these men.

1. Watch. This man said, sir, that Don John the
Prince's brother was a villain.

Dog. Write down Prince John a villain. Why, this   40
is flat perjury, to call a prince's brother villain.

Bora. Master Constable—

Dog. Pray thee, fellow, peace. I do not like thy
look, I promise thee.

Sex. What heard you him say else?   45

2. Watch. Marry, that he had received a thousand
ducats of Don John for accusing the Lady Hero
wrongfully.

Dog. Flat burglary as ever was committed.

Verg. Yea, by the mass, that it is.   50

Sex. What else, fellow?

66. **opinioned:** pinioned; fettered.
69. **God's my life:** God save me.
71. **naughty:** wicked.
74. **suspect:** respect.

1. Watch. And that Count Claudio did mean, upon his words, to disgrace Hero before the whole assembly and not marry her.

Dog. O villain! thou wilt be condemned into ever-   55
lasting redemption for this.

Sex. What else?

Watchmen. This is all.

Sex. And this is more, masters, than you can deny. Prince John is this morning secretly stol'n away. Hero   60
was in this manner accused, in this very manner re-
fused, and upon the grief of this suddenly died. Master Constable, let these men be bound and brought to Leonato's. I will go before and show him their examination.   [*Exit.*]   65

Dog. Come, let them be opinioned.

Verg. Let them be, in the hands—

Con. Off, coxcomb!

Dog. God's my life, where's the sexton? Let him write down the Prince's officer coxcomb. Come, bind   70
them—Thou naughty varlet!

Con. Away! you are an ass, you are an ass.

Dog. Dost thou not suspect my place? Dost thou not suspect my years? O that he were here to write me down an ass! But, masters, remember that I am an   75
ass. Though it be not written down, yet forget not that I am an ass. No, thou villain, thou art full of piety, as shall be proved upon thee by good witness. I am a wise fellow; and which is more, an officer; and which is more, a householder; and which is more, as pretty   80
a piece of flesh as any is in Messina, and one that knows the law, go to! and a rich fellow enough, go to!

and a fellow that hath had losses; and one that hath
two gowns and everything handsome about him. Bring
him away. O that I had been writ down an ass!   85

Exeunt.

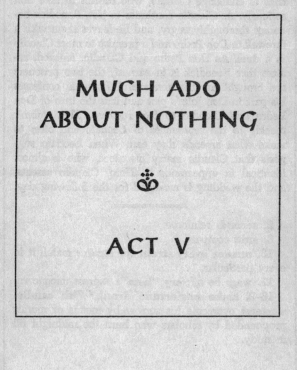

MUCH ADO
ABOUT NOTHING

❧

ACT V

V. [i.] Leonato's brother Antonio vainly attempts to comfort him. When Don Pedro and Claudio appear, the two old men assail them bitterly but cannot provoke them to fight. Benedick joins them and tries to challenge Claudio, who refuses to take him seriously. As Claudio continues to jest, Benedick becomes thoroughly angry, and he leaves them with a farewell to Don Pedro and a promise to meet Claudio in a duel. As Don Pedro and Claudio, amazed, realize that Benedick is in earnest, the two prisoners are brought in. The remorseful Borachio confesses his part in Don John's plot and it is the turn of Don Pedro and Claudio to feel remorse. They submit meekly to the reproaches of Leonato and offer to make what amends they can. When Leonato suggests that Claudio marry his niece, who is almost identical in appearance to Hero, Claudio assents, and the wedding is arranged for the following day.

━━━━━━━━━━━━━━━━━━━━━━

2. **second:** reinforce.

8. **suit:** compare.

13. **answer every strain for strain:** match it in every particular.

17. **wag:** be off; **cry "hem":** express unconcern.

18–9. **make misfortune drunk/With candle-wasters:** overcome his sorrow by means of morals propounded by scholars who burn the midnight oil in study.

ACT V

[Scene I. Before Leonato's house.]

Enter Leonato and his brother [Antonio].

Ant. If you go on thus, you will kill yourself,
And 'tis not wisdom thus to second grief
Against yourself.
Leon. I pray thee cease thy counsel,
Which falls into mine ears as profitless   5
As water in a sieve. Give not me counsel,
Nor let no comforter delight mine ear
But such a one whose wrongs do suit with mine.
Bring me a father that so loved his child,
Whose joy of her so overwhelmed like mine,   10
And bid him speak of patience.
Measure his woe the length and breadth of mine,
And let it answer every strain for strain,
As thus for thus, and such a grief for such,
In every lineament, branch, shape, and form.   15
If such a one will smile and stroke his beard,
Bid sorrow wag, cry "hem" when he should groan,
Patch grief with proverbs, make misfortune drunk
With candle-wasters—bring him yet to me,
And I of him will gather patience.   20

25. **preceptial medicine:** comfort in the form of precepts.

28. **'Tis all men's office:** i.e., every man undertakes the responsibility.

29. **wring:** writhe.

30. **sufficiency:** capability.

33. **cry louder than advertisement:** (1) are more potent than advice; (2) outdo the town-crier in noise.

39. **made a push at chance and sufferance:** defied misfortune and suffering.

But there is no such man; for, brother, men
Can counsel and speak comfort to that grief
Which they themselves not feel; but, tasting it,
Their counsel turns to passion, which before
Would give preceptial medicine to rage,   25
Fetter strong madness in a silken thread,
Charm ache with air and agony with words.
No, no! 'Tis all men's office to speak patience
To those that wring under the load of sorrow,
But no man's virtue nor sufficiency   30
To be so moral when he shall endure
The like himself. Therefore give me no counsel.
My griefs cry louder than advertisement.

   Ant. Therein do men from children nothing differ.

   Leon. I pray thee peace. I will be flesh and blood; 35
For there was never yet philosopher
That could endure the toothache patiently,
However they have writ the style of gods
And made a push at chance and sufferance.

   Ant. Yet bend not all the harm upon yourself. 40
Make those that do offend you suffer too.

   Leon. There thou speakst reason. Nay, I will do so.
My soul doth tell me Hero is belied;
And that shall Claudio know; so shall the Prince,
And all of them that thus dishonor her.   45

      Enter Don Pedro and Claudio.

   Ant. Here comes the Prince and Claudio hastily.

   Pedro. Good-den, good-den.

   Claud.   Good day to both of you.

53. **all is one:** no matter.

62. **beshrew:** plague take.

64. **meant nothing to my sword:** i.e., did not touch my sword deliberately.

69. **head:** face.

TERZA
QVINTA GVARDIA STRETTA,
difensiua, perfetta; nata da meza punta sopra-
mano, offensiua, da cui nasce un mezo
rouescio tondo.

A fencing thrust. From Angelo Vizani, *Trattato dello schermo* (1588).

Leon. Hear you, my lords!

Pedro. 　　　　　　We have some haste, Leonato. 50

Leon. Some haste, my lord! well, fare you well, my
　lord.

Are you so hasty now? Well, all is one.

Pedro. Nay, do not quarrel with us, good old man.

Ant. If he could right himself with quarreling, 55
Some of us would lie low.

Claud. 　　　　　　Who wrongs him?

Leon. Marry, thou dost wrong me, thou dissembler,
　thou!

Nay, never lay thy hand upon thy sword; 60
I fear thee not.

Claud. 　　　Marry, beshrew my hand
If it should give your age such cause of fear.
In faith, my hand meant nothing to my sword.

Leon. Tush, tush, man! never fleer and jest at me. 65
I speak not like a dotard nor a fool,
As under privilege of age to brag
What I have done being young, or what would do,
Were I not old. Know, Claudio, to thy head,
Thou hast so wronged mine innocent child and me 70
That I am forced to lay my reverence by
And, with gray hairs and bruise of many days,
Do challenge thee to trial of a man.
I say thou hast belied mine innocent child;
Thy slander hath gone through and through her heart, 75
And she lies buried with her ancestors—
O, in a tomb where never scandal slept,
Save this of hers, framed by thy villainy!

Claud. My villainy?

84. **nice fence:** skill in fencing.

86. **have to do with:** quarrel with.

87. **daff me:** brush me off.

92. **Win me and wear me:** a proverbial challenge; **answer me:** respond to my challenge.

94. **whip you from your foining fence:** repel your thrusts with a mere whip.

97. **Content yourself:** don't worry, leave this to me.

101. **apes:** jackanapes; upstarts; **Jacks:** impertinent knaves.

105. **scruple:** minute amount.

106. **Scambling:** belligerent; **outfacing:** impudent; **fashion-monging:** foppish.

107. **cog:** cheat.

108. **anticly:** like buffoons; **show outward hideousness:** make a pretense of being fearsome.

Leon.   Thine, Claudio; thine I say.   80
Pedro. You say not right, old man.
Leon.   My lord, my lord,
I'll prove it on his body if he dare,
Despite his nice fence and his active practice,
His May of youth and bloom of lustihood.   85
   Claud. Away! I will not have to do with you.
   Leon. Canst thou so daff me? Thou hast killed my
      child.
If thou killst me, boy, thou shalt kill a man.
   Ant. He shall kill two of us, and men indeed.   90
But that's no matter; let him kill one first.
Win me and wear me! Let him answer me.
Come, follow me, boy. Come, sir boy, come follow me.
Sir boy, I'll whip you from your foining fence!
Nay, as I am a gentleman, I will.   95
   Leon. Brother—
   Ant. Content yourself. God knows I loved my niece,
And she is dead, slandered to death by villains
That dare as well answer a man indeed
As I dare take a serpent by the tongue.   100
Boys, apes, braggarts, Jacks, milksops!
   Leon.   Brother Anthony—
   Ant. Hold you content. What, man! I know them,
      yea,
And what they weigh, even to the utmost scruple,   105
Scambling, outfacing, fashion-monging boys,
That lie and cog and flout, deprave and slander,
Go anticly, show outward hideousness,
And speak off half a dozen dang'rous words,

113. **'tis no matter:** don't concern yourself.

123. **And shall:** indeed we shall.

S.D. **ambo:** both (Latin).

128-29. **You are almost come to part almost a fray:** you have almost come in time to prevent what was almost a fray, echoing the proverb "Better come at the latter end of a feast than the beginning of a fray."

130. **We had like to have had:** we almost had.

133. **doubt:** fear.

135. **false:** unjustified.

How they might hurt their enemies, if they durst;   110
And this is all.

    Leon. But, brother Anthony—

    Ant.   Come, 'tis no matter.
Do not you meddle; let me deal in this.

    Pedro. Gentlemen both, we will not wake your   115
      patience.
My heart is sorry for your daughter's death;
But, on my honor, she was charged with nothing
But what was true and very full of proof.

    Leon. My lord, my lord—   120

    Pedro. I will not hear you.

    Leon. No? Come, brother, away!—I will be heard.

    Ant. And shall, or some of us will smart for it.

                             Exeunt ambo.

Enter Benedick.

    Pedro. See, see! Here comes the man we went to
      seek.   125

    Claud. Now, signior, what news?

    Bene. Good day, my lord.

    Pedro. Welcome, signior. You are almost come to
part almost a fray.

    Claud. We had like to have had our noses snapped   130
off with two old men without teeth.

    Pedro. Leonato and his brother. What thinkst thou?
Had we fought, I doubt we should have been too
young for them.

    Bene. In a false quarrel there is no true valor. I   135
came to seek you both.

138. **high-proof:** acutely.

143–44. **as we do the minstrels:** as we bid a musician draw his bow across his instrument.

148. **mettle:** fiery spirit.

150. **in the career:** as it gallops. A **career** is the headlong gallop of a horse.

157. **he knows how to turn his girdle:** "you may turn your girdle" was a phrase expressing a readiness to fight.

161. **make it good:** prove it.

162. **Do me right:** meet my challenge.

166–67. **so I may have good cheer:** provided you offer good food. Claudio refuses to take the challenge seriously.

A challenge. From Achille Marozzo, *Arte dell' armi* (1568).

Claud. We have been up and down to seek thee;
for we are high-proof melancholy and would fain have
it beaten away. Wilt thou use thy wit?

Bene. It is in my scabbard. Shall I draw it?   140

Pedro. Dost thou wear thy wit by thy side?

Claud. Never any did so, though very many have
been beside their wit. I will bid thee draw, as we do
the minstrels: draw to pleasure us.

Pedro. As I am an honest man, he looks pale. Art   145
thou sick or angry?

Claud. What, courage, man! What though care
killed a cat, thou hast mettle enough in thee to kill
care.

Bene. Sir, I shall meet your wit in the career, and   150
you charge it against me. I pray you choose another
subject.

Claud. Nay then, give him another staff; this last
was broke cross.

Pedro. By this light, he changes more and more. I   155
think he be angry indeed.

Claud. If he be, he knows how to turn his girdle.

Bene. Shall I speak a word in your ear?

Claud. God bless me from a challenge!

Bene. [*Aside to Claudio*] You are a villain. I jest   160
not; I will make it good how you dare, with what you
dare, and when you dare. Do me right, or I will protest your cowardice. You have killed a sweet lady, and
her death shall fall heavy on you. Let me hear from
you.   165

Claud. Well, I will meet you, so I may have good
cheer.

170. **calve's head:** fool.

171. **curiously:** skillfully.

172. **woodcock:** simpleton.

174. **praised:** appraised.

179–80. **a wise gentleman:** the implication is that a gentleman's wisdom is slight.

186. **proper'st:** handsomest.

189. **an if:** if.

192–93. **God saw him when he was hid in the garden:** as God saw Adam in the Garden of Eden when he tried to conceal himself, so Benedick was observed as he hid himself to eavesdrop on the conversation about Beatrice.

194–95. **set the savage bull's horns on the sensible Benedick's head:** referring to Benedick's rash statement at I. i. 253–58.

Pedro. What, a feast? a feast?

Claud. I' faith, I thank him, he hath bid me to a calve's head and a capon, the which if I do not carve 170 most curiously, say my knife's naught. Shall I not find a woodcock too?

Bene. Sir, your wit ambles well; it goes easily.

Pedro. I'll tell thee how Beatrice praised thy wit the other day. I said thou hadst a fine wit: "True," said 175 she, "a fine little one." "No," said I, "a great wit." "Right," says she, "a great gross one." "Nay," said I, "a good wit." "Just," said she, "it hurts nobody." "Nay," said I, "the gentleman is wise." "Certain," said she, "a wise gentleman." "Nay," said I, "he hath the tongues." 180 "That I believe," said she, "for he swore a thing to me on Monday night which he forswore on Tuesday morning. There's a double tongue; there's two tongues." Thus did she an hour together transshape thy particular virtues. Yet at last she concluded with 185 a sigh thou wast the proper'st man in Italy.

Claud. For the which she wept heartily and said she cared not.

Pedro. Yea, that she did; but yet, for all that, an if she did not hate him deadly, she would love him 190 dearly. The old man's daughter told us all.

Claud. All, all! and moreover, God saw him when he was hid in the garden.

Pedro. But when shall we set the savage bull's horns on the sensible Benedick's head? 195

Claud. Yea, and text underneath, "Here dwells Benedick, the married man"?

Bene. Fare you well, boy; you know my mind. I will

199. **gossiplike:** prattling.

215. **doctor:** learned man.

216-17. **soft you:** slow down; **Pluck up, my heart, and be sad:** pull yourself in, my friend, and speak seriously.

219. **reasons:** legal cases.

leave you now to your gossiplike humor. You break
jests as braggarts do their blades, which, God be 200
thanked, hurt not. My lord, for your many courtesies
I thank you. I must discontinue your company. Your
brother the Bastard is fled from Messina. You have
among you killed a sweet and innocent lady. For my
Lord Lackbeard there, he and I shall meet; and till 205
then peace be with him.   [*Exit.*]

Pedro. He is in earnest.

Claud. In most profound earnest; and, I'll warrant
you, for the love of Beatrice.

Pedro. And hath challenged thee.   210

Claud. Most sincerely.

Pedro. What a pretty thing man is when he goes in
his doublet and hose and leaves off his wit!

*Enter Constables [Dogberry and Verges, with the
Watch, leading] Conrade and Borachio.*

Claud. He is then a giant to an ape; but then is an
ape a doctor to such a man.   215

Pedro. But, soft you, let me be! Pluck up, my heart,
and be sad! Did he not say my brother was fled?

Dog. Come you, sir. If justice cannot tame you, she
shall ne'er weigh more reasons in her balance. Nay, an
you be a cursing hypocrite once, you must be looked 220
to.

Pedro. How now? two of my brother's men bound?
Borachio one.

Claud. Hearken after their offense, my lord.

Pedro. Officers, what offense have these men done? 225

228. **slanders:** slanderers.

235. **in his own division:** in accordance with the arrangement of his statement.

236. **well suited:** expressed in suitable terms.

250. **seal:** confirm; certify.

251. **upon:** as the result of.

Dog. Marry, sir, they have committed false report; moreover, they have spoken untruths; secondarily, they are slanders; sixth and lastly, they have belied a lady; thirdly, they have verified unjust things; and to conclude, they are lying knaves.　　　230

Pedro. First, I ask thee what they have done; thirdly, I ask thee what's their offense; sixth and lastly, why they are committed; and to conclude, what you lay to their charge.

Claud. Rightly reasoned, and in his own division; 235 and by my troth there's one meaning well suited.

Pedro. Who have you offended, masters, that you are thus bound to your answer? This learned constable is too cunning to be understood. What's your offense?

Bora. Sweet Prince, let me go no farther to mine 240 answer. Do you hear me, and let this Count kill me. I have deceived even your very eyes. What your wisdoms could not discover, these shallow fools have brought to light, who in the night overheard me confessing to this man how Don John your brother in- 245 censed me to slander the Lady Hero; how you were brought into the orchard and saw me court Margaret in Hero's garments; how you disgraced her when you should marry her. My villainy they have upon record, which I had rather seal with my death than repeat 250 over to my shame. The lady is dead upon mine and my master's false accusation; and briefly, I desire nothing but the reward of a villain.

Pedro. Runs not this speech like iron through your
　　blood?　　　255

Claud. I have drunk poison whiles he uttered it.

259. composed and framed: entirely made up.
283. pray your patience: beg your indulgence.

Pedro. But did my brother set thee on to this?

Bora. Yea, and paid me richly for the practice of it.

Pedro. He is composed and framed of treachery,
And fled he is upon this villainy.   260

Claud. Sweet Hero, now thy image doth appear
In the rare semblance that I loved it first.

Dog. Come, bring away the plaintiffs. By this time
our sexton hath reformed Signior Leonato of the matter. And, masters, do not forget to specify, when time   265
and place shall serve, that I am an ass.

Verg. Here, here comes Master Signior Leonato,
and the sexton too.

Enter Leonato, his brother [Antonio], and the Sexton.

Leon. Which is the villain? Let me see his eyes,
That when I note another man like him   270
I may avoid him. Which of these is he?

Bora. If you would know your wronger, look on me.

Leon. Art thou the slave that with thy breath hast
       killed
Mine innocent child?   275

Bora.   Yea, even I alone.

Leon. No, not so, villain! thou beliest thyself.
Here stand a pair of honorable men—
A third is fled—that had a hand in it.
I thank you princes for my daughter's death.   280
Record it with your high and worthy deeds.
'Twas bravely done, if you bethink you of it.

Claud. I know not how to pray your patience;
Yet I must speak. Choose your revenge yourself;

294. **Possess:** inform.
308. **dispose:** you may dispose.
313. **packed:** confederate.

Impose me to what penance your invention   285
Can lay upon my sin. Yet sinned I not
But in mistaking.
   Pedro.   By my soul, nor I!
And yet, to satisfy this good old man,
I would bend under any heavy weight   290
That he'll enjoin me to.
   Leon. I cannot bid you bid my daughter live—
That were impossible; but I pray you both,
Possess the people in Messina here
How innocent she died; and if your love   295
Can labor aught in sad invention,
Hang her an epitaph upon her tomb,
And sing it to her bones—sing it tonight.
Tomorrow morning come you to my house,
And since you could not be my son-in-law,   300
Be yet my nephew. My brother hath a daughter,
Almost the copy of my child that's dead,
And she alone is heir to both of us.
Give her the right you should have giv'n her cousin,
And so dies my revenge.   305
   Claud.   O noble sir!
Your over-kindness doth wring tears from me.
I do embrace your offer; and dispose
For henceforth of poor Claudio.
   Leon. Tomorrow, then, I will expect your coming;   310
Tonight I take my leave. This naughty man
Shall face to face be brought to Margaret,
Who I believe was packed in all this wrong,
Hired to it by your brother.
   Bora.   No, by my soul, she was not;   315

319–20. **under white and black:** written down.

332. **God save the foundation:** a conventional thanks for alms received from a charitable organization.

339–40. **if a merry meeting may be wished, God prohibit it:** may God permit that we meet on a happier occasion.

Nor knew not what she did when she spoke to me;
But always hath been just and virtuous
In anything that I do know by her.

Dog. Moreover, sir, which indeed is not under white
and black, this plaintiff here, the offender, did call me 320
ass. I beseech you let it be rememb'red in his punishment. And also the watch heard them talk of one
Deformed. They say he wears a key in his ear, and a
lock hanging by it, and borrows money in God's name,
the which he hath used so long and never paid that 325
now men grow hard-hearted and will lend nothing for
God's sake. Pray you examine him upon that point.

Leon. I thank thee for thy care and honest pains.

Dog. Your Worship speaks like a most thankful and
reverent youth, and I praise God for you.   330

Leon. There's for thy pains.   [*Gives money.*]

Dog. God save the foundation!

Leon. Go, I discharge thee of thy prisoner, and I
thank thee.

Dog. I leave an arrant knave with your Worship, 335
which I beseech your Worship to correct yourself, for
the example of others. God keep your Worship! I wish
your Worship well. God restore you to health! I
humbly give you leave to depart; and if a merry
meeting may be wished, God prohibit it! Come, neigh- 340
bor.   *Exeunt* [*Dogberry and Verges*].

Leon. Until tomorrow morning, lords, farewell.

Ant. Farewell, my lords. We look for you tomorrow.

Pedro. We will not fail.

Claud.   Tonight I'll mourn with Hero. 345
                    [*Exeunt Don Pedro and Claudio.*]

348. **lewd:** base (rather than lascivious).

——————————————————————————

V. [ii.] Benedick makes an effort to behave like the conventional lover by writing a sonnet to Beatrice, but he is interrupted by the lady herself. Although their love has been acknowledged, neither can quite abandon the old habit of verbal sparring. Ursula ends their conversation with the news that Hero has been exonerated, and they hasten to Leonato's to learn the details.

——————————————————————————

7. **come over it:** top it (with a pun on style/stile).
16–7. **give thee the bucklers:** present myself undefended by any shield.

Leon. [*To the Watch*] Bring you these fellows on.
—We'll talk with Margaret,
How her acquaintance grew with this lewd fellow.
                                   Exeunt.

[Scene II. Leonato's orchard.]

Enter Benedick and Margaret.

Bene. Pray thee, sweet Mistress Margaret, deserve
well at my hands by helping me to the speech of
Beatrice.

Marg. Will you then write me a sonnet in praise of
my beauty?   5

Bene. In so high a style, Margaret, that no man living shall come over it; for, in most comely truth, thou
deservest it.

Marg. To have no man come over me? Why, shall
I always keep belowstairs?   10

Bene. Thy wit is as quick as the greyhound's
mouth: it catches.

Marg. And yours as blunt as the fencer's foils, which
hit but hurt not.

Bene. A most manly wit, Margaret: it will not hurt   15
a woman. And so I pray thee call Beatrice. I give thee
the bucklers.

Marg. Give us the swords; we have bucklers of our
own.

Bene. If you use them, Margaret, you must put in   20

21. **pikes:** bucklers commonly had spikes in the center.

30. **Leander:** the lover of Hero, who swam the Hellespont nightly to see her.

31. **panders:** Troilus was assisted in his wooing of Cressida by her uncle, Pandarus, who gave his name to the term "pander."

32. **quondam:** onetime; **carpet-mongers:** carpet-knights; pseudo-gallants of no true valor or devotion in comparison with himself.

Leander swimming the Hellespont. From Musaeus, *Opusculum de Herone & Leandro* (1538).

the pikes with a vice, and they are dangerous
weapons for maids.

Marg. Well, I will call Beatrice to you, who I think
hath legs.

Bene. And therefore will come.   *Exit Margaret.*   25

[Sings]   The god of love,
                That sits above
            And knows me, and knows me,
                How pitiful I deserve—

I mean in singing; but in loving, Leander the good   30
swimmer, Troilus the first employer of panders, and a
whole book full of these quondam carpet-mongers,
whose names yet run smoothly in the even road of a
blank verse—why, they were never so truly turned
over and over as my poor self in love. Marry, I cannot   35
show it in rhyme. I have tried. I can find out no rhyme
to "lady" but "baby"—an innocent rhyme; for "scorn,"
"horn"—a hard rhyme; for "school," "fool"—a babbling
rhyme: very ominous endings! No, I was not born
under a rhyming planet, nor I cannot woo in festival   40
terms.

Enter Beatrice.

Sweet Beatrice, wouldst thou come when I called
thee?

Beat. Yea, signior, and depart when you bid me.

Bene. O, stay but till then!   45

57. **subscribe him:** write him down.

61. **politic:** artfully contrived.

70. **It appears not in this confession:** i.e., if Benedick were truly wise, he would not claim wisdom.

72–3. **instance:** example; **lived in the time of good neighbors:** i.e., in former days, when a man's neighbor would praise him, self-praise was properly condemned.

Beat. "Then" is spoken. Fare you well now. And yet, ere I go, let me go with that I came for, which is, with knowing what hath passed between you and Claudio.

Bene. Only foul words; and thereupon I will kiss thee.   50

Beat. Foul words is but foul wind, and foul wind is but foul breath, and foul breath is noisome. Therefore I will depart unkissed.

Bene. Thou hast frighted the word out of his right sense, so forcible is thy wit. But I must tell thee   55
plainly, Claudio undergoes my challenge; and either I must shortly hear from him or I will subscribe him a coward. And I pray thee now tell me, for which of my bad parts didst thou first fall in love with me?

Beat. For them all together, which maintained so   60
politic a state of evil that they will not admit any good part to intermingle with them. But for which of my good parts did you first suffer love for me?

Bene. Suffer love!—a good epithet. I do suffer love indeed, for I love thee against my will.   65

Beat. In spite of your heart, I think. Alas, poor heart! If you spite it for my sake, I will spite it for yours, for I will never love that which my friend hates.

Bene. Thou and I are too wise to woo peaceably.

Beat. It appears not in this confession. There's not   70
one wise man among twenty that will praise himself.

Bene. An old, an old instance, Beatrice, that lived in the time of good neighbors. If a man do not erect in this age his own tomb ere he dies, he shall live no longer in monument than the bell rings and the widow   75
weeps.

91. **old coil:** a great commotion.
93. **abused:** deceived.

Beat. And how long is that, think you?

Bene. Question: why, an hour in clamor and a quarter in rheum. Therefore is it most expedient for the wise, if Don Worm (his conscience) find no impediment to the contrary, to be the trumpet of his own virtues, as I am to myself. So much for praising myself, who, I myself will bear witness, is praiseworthy. And now tell me, how doth your cousin?

Beat. Very ill.

Bene. And how do you?

Beat. Very ill too.

Bene. Serve God, love me, and mend. There will I leave you too, for here comes one in haste.

Enter Ursula.

Urs. Madam, you must come to your uncle. Yonder's old coil at home. It is proved my Lady Hero hath been falsely accused, the Prince and Claudio mightily abused, and Don John is the author of all, who is fled and gone. Will you come presently?

Beat. Will you go hear this news, signior?

Bene. I will live in thy heart, die in thy lap, and be buried in thy eyes; and moreover, I will go with thee to thy uncle's.

Exeunt.

V. [iii.] The penitent Claudio places a memorial epitaph on the monument where Hero's body supposedly rests and promises to perform yearly rites in her honor. He and Don Pedro are then to clothe themselves for the wedding at Leonato's.

▬▬▬▬▬▬▬▬▬▬▬▬▬

5. **guerdon:** recompense.
12. **goddess of the night:** the moon-goddess Diana.

[Scene III. A church.]

Enter Claudio, Don Pedro, and three or four with tapers, [followed by Musicians].

Claud. Is this the monument of Leonato?
Lord. It is, my lord.
Claud. [*Reads from a scroll*]

Epitaph.

Done to death by slanderous tongues
    Was the Hero that here lies.
Death, in guerdon of her wrongs,   5
    Gives her fame which never dies.
So the life that died with shame
Lives in death with glorious fame.

Hang thou there upon the tomb,
                     [*Hangs up the scroll.*]
Praising her when I am dumb.   10
Now, music, sound, and sing your solemn hymn.

Song.

Pardon, goddess of the night,
Those that slew thy virgin knight;
For the which, with songs of woe,
Round about her tomb they go.

26. **Phoebus:** Phoebus Apollo, the sun-god.

30. **weeds:** garments.

32. **Hymen:** god of marriage; **speed's:** speed us; i.e., give us a fortunate outcome.

V. [iv.] Leonato's household awaits the arrival of Claudio and Don Pedro, and Benedick takes the opportunity of arranging for his marriage to Beatrice. Hero is presented to Claudio disguised, but when he takes her hand, she removes her mask and explains that she had only died while her name was dishonored. After this happy revelation, Benedick and Beatrice discover their mutual mistake in thinking the other was pining for love, but both are satisfied with the outcome and Benedick calls for a dance before the marriage ceremony.

Midnight, assist our moan,
Help us to sigh and groan
   Heavily, heavily.
Graves, yawn and yield your dead,
Till death be uttered   20
   Heavily, heavily.

Claud. Now unto thy bones good night!
    Yearly will I do this rite.
Pedro. Good morrow, masters. Put your torches out.
The wolves have preyed, and look, the gentle day,   25
Before the wheels of Phoebus, round about
Dapples the drowsy East with spots of grey.
Thanks to you all, and leave us. Fare you well.
   Claud. Good morrow, masters. Each his several way.
   Pedro. Come, let us hence and put on other weeds,   30
And then to Leonato's we will go.
   Claud. And Hymen now with luckier issue speed's
Than this for whom we rend'red up this woe.
                       Exeunt.

[Scene IV. A room in Leonato's house.]

Enter Leonato, Benedick, [Beatrice,] Margaret,
Ursula, Antonio, Friar, Hero.

Friar. Did I not tell you she was innocent?
Leon. So are the Prince and Claudio, who accused
  her

7. **question:** investigation.

9. **faith:** faithfulness to his vow.

18. **confirmed countenance:** convincing show of sincerity.

30. **stand:** agree.

Phoebus Apollo in his chariot. From Robert Whitcombe, *Janua divorum* (1678).

Upon the error that you heard debated.
But Margaret was in some fault for this,   5
Although against her will, as it appears
In the true course of all the question.

   Ant. Well, I am glad that all things sort so well.

   Bene. And so am I, being else by faith enforced
To call young Claudio to a reckoning for it.   10

   Leon. Well, daughter, and you gentlewomen all,
Withdraw into a chamber by yourselves,
And, when I send for you, come hither masked.

                           Exeunt Ladies.

The Prince and Claudio promised by this hour
To visit me. You know your office, brother: 15
You must be father to your brother's daughter,
And give her to young Claudio.

   Ant. Which I will do with confirmed countenance.

   Bene. Friar, I must entreat your pains, I think.

   Friar. To do what, signior?   20

   Bene. To bind me, or undo me—one of them.
Signior Leonato, truth it is, good signior,
Your niece regards me with an eye of favor.

   Leon. That eye my daughter lent her. 'Tis most true.

   Bene. And I do with an eye of love requite her.   25

   Leon. The sight whereof I think you had from me,
From Claudio, and the Prince; but what's your will?

   Bene. Your answer, sir, is enigmatical;
But, for my will, my will is, your good will
May stand with ours, this day to be conjoined   30
In the state of honorable marriage;
In which, good friar, I shall desire your help.

50. play the noble beast: Jove disguised himself as a bull to abduct Europa.

55. For this I owe you: i.e., I must wait to answer your jest another time.

The rape of Europa. From Gabriel Simeoni, *La vita et Metamorfoseo d'Ovidio* (1559).

Leon. My heart is with your liking.
Friar.   And my help.

Enter Don Pedro and Claudio and two or three other.

Here comes the Prince and Claudio.   35
　Pedro. Good morrow to this fair assembly.
　Leon. Good morrow, Prince; good morrow, Claudio.
We here attend you. Are you yet determined
Today to marry with my brother's daughter?
　Claud. I'll hold my mind, were she an Ethiope.   40
　Leon. Call her forth, brother. Here's the friar ready.
                              [*Exit Antonio.*]
　Pedro. Good morrow, Benedick. Why, what's the
　　matter   ˙
That you have such a February face,
So full of frost, of storm, and cloudiness?   45
　Claud. I think he thinks upon the savage bull.
Tush, fear not, man! We'll tip thy horns with gold,
And all Europa shall rejoice at thee,
As once Europa did at lusty Jove
When he would play the noble beast in love.   50
　Bene. Bull Jove, sir, had an amiable low,
And some such strange bull leaped your father's cow
And got a calf in that same noble feat
Much like to you, for you have just his bleat.

*Enter [Leonato's] brother [Antonio], Hero, Beatrice,
　Margaret, Ursula, [the ladies wearing masks].*

　Claud. For this I owe you. Here comes other   55
　　reck'nings.

74. **qualify:** reduce.

76. **largely:** in full.

77. **let wonder seem familiar:** accept these remarkable events as though they were commonplaces.

79. **Soft and fair:** slowly and smoothly, an admonition not to rush matters without proper explanation.

Which is the lady I must seize upon?

  Ant. This same is she, and I do give you her.

  Claud. Why then, she's mine. Sweet, let me see your
    face. 60

  Leon. No, that you shall not till you take her hand

Before this friar and swear to marry her.

  Claud. Give me your hand before this holy friar.

I am your husband if you like of me.

  Hero. And when I lived I was your other wife; 65
                      [*Unmasks.*]

And when you loved you were my other husband.

  Claud. Another Hero!

  Hero.   Nothing certainer.

One Hero died defiled; but I do live,

And surely as I live, I am a maid. 70

  Pedro. The former Hero! Hero that is dead!

  Leon. She died, my lord, but whiles her slander
    lived.

  Friar. All this amazement can I qualify,

When, after that the holy rites are ended, 75

I'll tell you largely of fair Hero's death.

Meantime let wonder seem familiar,

And to the chapel let us presently.

  Bene. Soft and fair, friar. Which is Beatrice?

  Beat. [*Unmasks*] I answer to that name. What is 80
    your will?

  Bene. Do not you love me?

  Beat.   Why, no; no more than reason.

  Bene. Why, then your uncle, and the Prince, and
    Claudio 85

Have been deceived; they swore you did.

115–17. **If a man will be beaten with brains, 'a shall wear nothing handsome about him:** a man that can be vanquished by another's wit will never be able to protect his person.

Beat. Do not you love me?

Bene.   Troth, no; no more than reason.

Beat. Why, then my cousin, Margaret, and Ursula
Are much deceived; for they did swear you did.   90

Bene. They swore that you were almost sick for me.

Beat. They swore that you were well-nigh dead for
   me.

Bene. 'Tis no such matter. Then you do not love me?

Beat. No, truly, but in friendly recompense.   95

Leon. Come, cousin, I am sure you love the gentleman.

Claud. And I'll be sworn upon't that he loves her;
For here's a paper written in his hand,
A halting sonnet of his own pure brain,   100
Fashioned to Beatrice.

Hero.   And here's another,
Writ in my cousin's hand, stol'n from her pocket,
Containing her affection unto Benedick.

Bene. A miracle! Here's our own hands against our   105
hearts. Come, I will have thee; but, by this light, I
take thee for pity.

Beat. I would not deny you; but, by this good day,
I yield upon great persuasion, and partly to save your
life, for I was told you were in a consumption.   110

Bene. Peace! I will stop your mouth.   [*Kisses her.*]

Pedro. How dost thou, Benedick, the married man?

Bene. I'll tell thee what, Prince: a college of wit-
crackers cannot flout me out of my humor. Dost thou
think I care for a satire or an epigram? No. If a man 115
will be beaten with brains, 'a shall wear nothing handsome about him. In brief, since I do purpose to marry,

121. **conclusion:** final decision.

127–28. **look exceeding narrowly to thee:** watch thee very closely.

133. **First, of my word:** by my word, let's have dancing first.

135. **reverent:** honorable.

I will think nothing to any purpose that the world can
say against it; and therefore never flout at me for what
I have said against it; for man is a giddy thing, and 120
this is my conclusion. For thy part, Claudio, I did
think to have beaten thee; but in that thou art like to
be my kinsman, live unbruised and love my cousin.

Claud. I had well hoped thou wouldst have denied
Beatrice, that I might have cudgeled thee out of thy 125
single life, to make thee a double-dealer, which out of
question thou wilt be if my cousin do not look exceeding narrowly to thee.

Bene. Come, come, we are friends. Let's have a
dance ere we are married, that we may lighten our 130
own hearts and our wives' heels.

Leon. We'll have dancing afterward.

Bene. First, of my word! Therefore play, music.
Prince, thou art sad. Get thee a wife, get thee a wife!
There is no staff more reverent than one tipped with 135
horn.

Enter Messenger.

Mess. My lord, your brother John is ta'en in flight,
And brought with armed men back to Messina.

Bene. Think not on him till tomorrow. I'll devise
thee brave punishments for him. Strike up, pipers! 140

Dance.

[Exeunt.]

He hath indeed better bett'red expectation than you must expect of me to tell you how. [*Messenger*—I. i. 15-7]

How much better is it to weep at joy than to joy at weeping! [*Leonato*—I. i. 27-8]

He is a very valiant trencherman. [*Beatrice*—I. i. 49]

The gentleman is not in your books. [*Messenger*—I. i. 74-5]

Benedick the married man. [*Benedick*—I. i. 258]

As merry as the day is long. [*Beatrice*—II. i. 46]

Speak low, if you speak love. [*Don Pedro*—II.i. 92]

It keeps on the windy side of care. [*Beatrice*—II. i. 298-99]

I was born to speak all mirth and no matter. [*Beatrice*—II. i. 313-14]

I will tell you my drift. [*Don Pedro*—II. i. 369]

He was wont to speak plain and to the purpose. [*Benedick*—II. iii. 17-8]

He hath a heart as sound as a bell. [*Don Pedro*—III. ii. 11-2]

Are you good men and true? [*Dogberry*—III. iii. 1]

You may say they are not the men you took them for. [*Dogberry*—III. iii. 46-7]

They that touch pitch will be defiled. [*Dogberry*—III. iii. 56]

Not for the wide world! [*Benedick*—IV. i. 310]

There was never yet philosopher
That could endure the toothache patiently. [*Leonato*—V. i. 36-7]

Some of us will smart for it. [*Antonio*—V. i. 123]

What though care killed a cat, thou hast mettle enough in thee to kill care. [*Claudio*—V. i. 147-49]

I was not born under a rhyming planet. [*Benedick*—V. ii. 39-40]